BOUND

Book 2 of A New Life Series

Samantha Jacobey

ISBN: **0692024360**
ISBN-13: **978-0692024362**

Bound

Book 2 of A New Life Series

Samantha Jacobey

Lavish Publishing, LLC ~ Houston

First Edition
2015 Lavish Publishing, LLC
Book 2 of A New Life Series
All Rights Reserved
Published in the United States by Lavish Publishing, LLC, Houston
Cover Design by: Nicolene Lorette Design
Cover Images: SHUTTERSTOCK
Paperback ISBN
ISBN: **0692024360**
ISBN-13: **978-0692024362**
www.LavishPublishing.com

.

Table of Contents

Prologue

Special Agent Eli Founder sat on his bed, staring at the small volume of German Fairytales. He had retrieved it from the hospital for her, and intended to place it inside the suitcase with her belongings, a special message penned on the first few pages.

The problem was, he had been about the task for over an hour and was still torn with what he should write. The girl had moved him in a way he had never expected, and although he could admit to himself that their relationship would more than likely end, it hurt. He wanted the chance to let it play out, regardless of where it led. He wanted the chance to love her. Most of all, he wanted to cling to the possibility that they would have more time.

Running his fingers through his coal black hair, he spoke out loud, despite the fact that he was alone in the apartment. "You better suck it up, big boy. In the end, this comes down to one thing. You've still got a job to do. And so does she…" His voice trailed away and he pulled the cap off of the felt tipped pen, scrawling in clean cursive:

My Dearest Tori,

I know the past was filled with difficult times, and your future feels uncertain. Understand that you are not alone in your quest and that even though your path will not be an easy one, you are strong, and you will endure, so long as you endeavor to persevere. My thoughts and hopes are with you.

7

Yours Always,
Eli

Give Me Wings

Tori could not stop the flutter of excitement as she scurried through the airport, nor the guilty feeling her anticipation produced. Special Agent Debra Paisley, who walked beside her, grabbed her arm, tugging her towards the correct gate.

Dodging people left and right, the pair moved quickly towards the ticket counter. "Flight eight-six-six, ORD to LAX, here we go!" Debra herself had become enthusiastic as the time of her young charge's departure drew closer, in a nervous motherly kind of way.

Tori looked around the crowded O'Hare in amazement, the number of gates and flights daunting. She felt very glad her new friend had come with her to make sure she made it to her flight. "Here hun, bring your bag." Debra led her over to the boarding area, and Tori had a mad rush of adrenaline as she realized she was actually getting on the plane.

Stopping abruptly, she latched onto her companion, terror in her eyes. Seeing the petrified look on her face, the older woman guided her over to the side, where a large window afforded a view of the loading areas and runways further beyond. "Just breathe," she instructed, "You're fine. We have a few minutes if you need them."

Tori felt grateful for her understanding, leaning her forehead against the glass and taking in slow deep breaths. Her friend and mentor rubbed her spine and smiled while giving her a pep talk in a low voice, "Try and relax.

Everything's fine. And it's going to be great once you get there."

Tori looked at her with tears brimming over in her crystal blue eyes. "I don't want to go," she stated with a slight whine. "You and Eli are the only friends I have. The only people I know. What the hell am I going to do in LA?" Things had been an emotional rollercoaster for the girl, only finding out the previous day that she was leaving, and would not see either of the only two people she cared about for at least six months.

Debra understood her apprehension, and hugged her close while stroking the girl's long dark hair. "Shhshh," she soothed. "You know Eli and I will be counting the days until our next meeting. We both will be there; we promise. But now you have to go, sweetheart. We have to give you wings and let you learn to fly."

Tori relaxed into the embrace, having conquered her fear of women and of allowing people to touch her out of hand. Then, remembering her makeup, she pulled away and began dabbing her eyes the way Debra had shown her, while blinking rapidly.

"There you go," the older woman smiled broadly, "That's exactly how you do it," trying to lift her spirits, but afraid in the end she would have to put her on the plane in tears.

Taking quick, ragged breaths, Tori knew her time was short. "Ok," she huffed, "I'm ready I think." Throwing her bag over her shoulder, she moved towards the entrance once more. Debra admired her courage and walked beside her right up to the gate. Holding out her boarding pass to the little man in the uniform, Tori gave her a faint smile and disappeared into the tunnel.

As soon as she was out of sight, Debra let her own tears begin to fall and made her way through the crowded passages towards the parking lot. *This was hard for everyone, baby girl*, she told herself as she trudged along, *but we will all make it through.*

Meanwhile, taking deep breaths, Tori admonished herself for turning into a pansy in such a short time. It used to be you could not make her cry, no matter how badly you hurt her. She would not give in or give you the satisfaction; back when she was tough.

She made her way through the tunnel and onto the plane, and another wave of panic hit her as she stepped through the door of the massive 747. Looking around, she stopped in awe of the aircraft's interior. Before her lay three columns of seats, and the chamber seemed enormous. Tori had never flown anywhere before, and became overcome by a strange combination of curiosity and fear. People pushed in behind her, so she moved forward, trying to locate her seat from the entry area.

Luckily, a flight attendant noticed her dazed expression and asked if she needed any help. Tori quickly wiped the damp spot under her eye and asked where her accommodations were located. The woman smiled in sympathy and led her straight to it. She had been assigned 57 B, so there would be a person on each side of her, but close enough to a window, she might be able to see out.

Stuffing her bag into the overhead compartment, Tori began to feel calmer. Remembering to pull out her notebook, she grabbed it and her pencil before sinking onto the cushion.

Dr. Carlisle had suggested that she keep a journal, so she planned on starting fresh with the flight, and wrote the date at the top of the first page. Then she made a note about her seat number. While she wrote, a couple arrived and announced they were the owners of the other two seats. She stared up at them as they asked if she would not mind moving one way or the other so they could sit together.

Grasping the opportunity, her dark curls bounced when

she leapt up to move over next to the window, and began to peer out of it eagerly. Her first flight and she would have a great seat for taking it all in, with only a small bundle of nerves tickling her stomach. Marking a single line through 57B, she changed it to 57A and wrote *window seat* next to it.

Tori watched as the plane filled, periodically peeking out the window to see if anything had changed outside. The couple seated next to her was obviously very passionate about one another, as they were kissing and petting one another quite heavily. The sight of them made her heart heavy, remembering Eli's bed and how comfortable she had been sharing it with him.

She felt relieved she had chosen the window and would have something else to draw her attention. Turning and placing the spiral so she could write more privately, she made a note about public displays of affection being annoying to her. Expressing her feelings on paper gave her feeling of vindication, and she managed a tiny smile to herself as she watched the carts roll around on the ground below.

At last, the door closed and everyone had their seat. An attendant stood at the front of the plane and began to give directions. Tucking a few ebony locks behind her ear, Tori leaned forward to listen more closely, catching something about emergency exits. She hadn't thought about the possibility of a crash; she could feel her heart rate jump as she strained to catch ever word.

She gripped the armrests on each side of her tightly when she felt the plane begin to roll. The guy sitting next to her glanced over from his lover and laughed. "Relax, babe. We aren't even in the air yet!" Giving him a worried glance, she tried to do as he instructed, leaning back against the headrest and taking deep breaths.

Folding her hands into her lap, she watched out the

window and could see the asphalt below the plane racing by. Tori felt a lurch, and then the saw the ground dropping beneath them, causing an odd sensation in her chest from the optical illusion it produced. Leaning towards the tiny window, she pressed her fingers against the glass in awe as they climbed, still feeling the undulation of thrill and terror in the pit of her stomach.

The plane tilted upwards for several minutes, and then leveled out. Still gazing out the window, she thought the ground looked like a giant quilt, with the blocks and sections pretty well defined, a repeating pattern of dark and light falling across them.

Soon after, another flight attendant came by pushing a large cart with drinks and snacks on it. Tori picked up a bottle of water to sip while she watched the world pass beneath her. Not wanting to witness the show to her right, she remained focused on the tiny portal to her left. Peering out into the horizon, she noted how everything began to get blurry before it disappeared.

She watched the clouds for a while. She looked over the parts of the wing she could see. Eventually, she had to admit, flying in a plane was pretty boring. *Not like riding on a bike with the wind in my face and the road whizzing by beneath me.* She sat drumming her fingers against the glass for a while, and began to replay the events of the last month or so in her mind. After a few minutes of reflection, she decided to write a brief summary in her journal. She wrote:

I woke up in Mercy Hospital in Chicago thirty-six days ago. I spent four days in the hospital portion, and then was sent over to the mental health ward for twenty-nine days. I spent two nights at the federal building and one night with Eli. In that short amount of time, my life has completely changed. I have gone from being the property of a group of mercenaries, living a life of pain and anguish, to a young

13

woman headed to a halfway house, a job, and a future. I have two friends, Eli Founder and Debra Paisley...

Special Agents Eli Founder and Debra Paisley had been assigned to her committee; a group of federal agents who were overseeing the acquisition of knowledge the girl possessed about several illegal organizations. They were also working towards formulating a plan to integrate her into a normal life.

Because actual proof of her age had not been available, Tori had been evaluated by Dr. Bennet, who determined her age to be under fifteen years. The girl had strongly contested his findings, but to no avail. She was currently on conditional release according to the terms of the agreement that the Feds had offered, and she had accepted. She had come to realize that all of that was the easy part, and the hard part lay ahead.

Tori pushed her hand against her chest; the folded yellow piece of paper in her pocket made a slight crinkle noise beneath the pressure. On it were two addresses—the halfway house and a music store. The first would be her home for the next six months. The second belonged to an old friend of Jim Godfry's, who had been in charge of the committee.

Jim had called in a favor to get her a job; he claimed the move would allow her to learn to support herself, but she suspected the real purpose had been so he could keep tabs on her. The girl had not been raised under the best of circumstances, and had proven she could be dangerous, even lethal, when she chose to be. *They don't trust me, and why should they?*

Just then, a red light came on behind the words *fasten seatbelt*, and Tori hoped that meant the journey had come to an end. Closing her notebook, she straightened in her seat and ensured her belt securely fastened. Watching out the window, she could see different parts of the wing moving, and that seemed somewhat interesting to her, or at least it distracted her from the fear of crashing while the plane descended.

She had read a book about planes once, so she knew the large parts that moved on the back were called flaps and were for landing. She looked for the smaller pieces out on the tip of the wing, called ailerons, which were used for steering, but wasn't so sure she could locate them on the enormous wing. She supposed these parts were run by hydraulics, which could be sabotaged if she were to ever want to disable a plane; *not that I'll have any need of such an idea, since my life is on a different path.*

A few minutes later, the aircraft touched down, taxied around to the gate and made an abrupt stop. Tori stood, along with everyone else, to grab items out of the storage bins overhead and pull purses from under seats. She could feel the butterflies bouncing around in her stomach; she wasn't in a hurry to get off the plane to meet a bunch of new people or to have to explain herself to anyone. Reluctantly, she made her way down the passage and out into the gate area.

Brandon knew the girl as soon as she exited the tunnel. *Wow, she's tall... very tall, gotta be at least six foot.* Her hair long and dark, almost black, she appeared quite stunning, but he recalled being told she had a very large scar on her face from her past life; *the makeup hides it well.*

Wearing jeans, boots and a black leather jacket, her white shirt peeking from underneath, she seemed quite cool and collected. She also did not look to be only fifteen years of age. Smiling broadly, he held out his hand to greet her, "Hi, I'm Brandon Tate. You must be Tori."

The girl looked down at the extended digits and felt her palms go sweaty. *So much for conquered fears.* Mentally, she tried to persuade herself to shake his hand, but in the end, she pursed her lips and moved her gaze back to his face; "I don't like to be touched."

15

A little surprised, Brandon withdrew his arm, his smile growing slightly strained. "Well then, let's head this way," he indicated their route in the most upbeat tone he could muster.

Walking through the crowd beside him, Tori threw her bag over her shoulder and pulled her sunglasses out of an inner pocket to slide them on. The Dragons had been to Cali quite a few times on business, so she was familiar with LA, as well as a few other major metropolitan areas.

She began to run down her mental checklist and refresh her memory on what she knew about the city and its people. They had some connections there, but Tori felt confident she would not need them; furthermore, she surmised using them could be dangerous.

Giving her a sideways glance, Brandon wondered exactly what was going on with her. He had been given little background by the federal officer who contacted him; very little, and he had the feeling it would be the parts they didn't mention that were going to matter most. *Oh well,* he sighed to himself. *We'll get her on track; after all that's what we do.*

Out loud, he asked if she had ever been to California or LA, to which she replied, "Yes, both."

He chuckled at her response, as he had also been told she didn't talk much, and there she had proved it. The pair continued without speaking until they reached his grey 2006 Toyota Corolla. The girl tossed her bag in the back seat, and they climbed inside.

Trying to make small talk, Brandon observed, "You travel light."

Tori remained silent, glaring out the window as they exited the airport. Mentally, she scoffed at his comment, as the bag held three or four times the personal property she had ever owned in the past. She had wanted to be positive about her time in the big city, but her enthusiasm had all but disappeared.

Pulling onto Lincoln Boulevard, he decided to get to the point, "So, you'll be staying with us for six months and then be released?"

She sighed, mumbling crossly, "That's the plan."

He continued by giving her the house rules; having spoken them many times, they rolled easily off his tongue. "Curfew is midnight. No fighting or fraternizing with other tenants. Clean up after yourself. Maintain your employment. Pay your rent on time. Attend your group sessions."

Tori's head snapped to face him. Perturbed, "What group sessions?" she demanded. "Eli said there wouldn't be any more stupid meetings with whiney ass people."

Brandon grinned at her response. "Attending meetings is a must. You can attend NA or AA, whichever you think is best for you. It'll help you figure out what's important and how to stay clean." He smiled encouragingly, but could tell she was not happy about the news.

Slowly turning back to her window, Tori fumed inside, and they rode the rest of the way without another word passing between them.

Half-way Home

Pulling into the driveway of a rather large, multilevel dwelling, Brandon announced they were home and cut off the engine. Tori peered out the window, not moving from the vehicle.

She could see a large porch that ran across a portion of the front and down the full side of the Victorian style house. There were bright orange trumpet vines hanging all across the veranda, shading it from the evening sun and prying eyes.

At the back of the driveway stood a single door garage. Tori contemplated she would be more comfortable in the small shack alone than the giant house full of people.

Brandon lifted her bag from the back seat, and then opened her door for her, standing patiently for her to decide to exit. Her eyes shifted up at him, her face stoic, she knew she had no choice but to comply, so she climbed out and scrutinized the house from the sidewalk.

Painted in shades of brown and deep mahogany, Tori could see it appeared to be peeling and cracked in places. "You need new paint," she observed aloud. Brandon agreed, pleased she had something to say.

Stepping up onto the veranda, the girl noted a large swing hanging at the far end and various chairs and tables scattered the full length to the corner on the front side. For a moment, she thought it would be a nice place to curl up with a book, then pushed the image away, resolute she did not want to get too comfortable there; *this's only a temporary stop.*

Moving inside, they arrived in a rather spacious kitchen area that opened up across a short bar into a large dining room. Together, they made up the back half of this side of the house, the kitchen ending at three-quarters of the way up.

Walking straight across, they entered a hallway that made up the heart of the structure. From there, you could go left and be at the entrance of the master suite, right and be in the living areas, or up the stairs to the tenant rooms above. For the moment, they moved to the right, towards the living room, where everyone had gathered to greet her.

The front door lay at the end of the hall, with a small foyer containing a coat rack and entry table, and a large square arch that served as the entryway into the open living area that took up one-fourth of the ground floor. Stopping beneath the wide beam, she could see that the room held a conversation group, with a sectional and oversized couch at the far end, and a flat-screened television and sitting area at the front end.

A fireplace in the center of the exterior wall divided the two sections, and a bay window hung out the front, which held a large seat with pillows to stretch out and enjoy the view. From what she had seen so far, the house probably appeared plain to other people, but having never lived in one before, to Tori it was a palace.

Looking over her left shoulder, there stood the open door of what appeared to be an office that took up the rest of the house on the ground floor between the kitchen wall and the exterior. Back down the hall, the stairs to the next level hugged the right hand wall, the half bath for the ground floor hidden underneath.

She allowed a deep sigh to escape her as she remembered that she was stuck there, and found herself longing for the feel of a breeze and the rustle of tree leaves above her. Turning back into the large living area, she continued inside to be introduced to her new roommates.

Brandon started with Sharon, his wife and co-manager of the house. Her round face smiled warmly, while she flipped her long straight auburn locks over her shoulder.

Moving around the room, Robert looked to be about forty-ish with dark hair curling around his balding dome and a bushy beard and mustache combo. He smiled as well and stepped forward, offering his hand, which Brandon quickly headed off with a short, "She doesn't like to be touched," for her.

Curling the outstretched fingers into a brief fist, he settled for a small wave, "Call me Bob."

The rest of the group seemed less appreciative of the new tenant, as Richard gave her a long dull-eyed stare, shifting his gaze up and down her tall frame. Jonathon held a phone in his hand and barely looked up from his finger sliding as he was mentioned.

Lindsey, who sat propped up on the oversized couch, gave her a scowl, "Do you always dress like that?" The small blonde had been excited to hear another girl was coming to the house, and did not hide her disappointment at who had actually arrived.

Tori took note of their reactions, not bothering to smile. She could feel the walls of protection that she had so carefully constructed as a Dragon closing in around her; using these, she would keep them all at bay, and her secrets safely hidden.

At last, Brandon asked Sharon if she wanted to show their newest resident upstairs, to which the older woman smiled her agreement and led the way. On the way up, she explained that each floor had its own full bathroom with a shower and tub combo, as well as a three-quarter bath with shower only. The second floor was dedicated to women and the third floor being the men's level.

The rooms were arranged in a simple grid, each corner being a bedroom with a bathroom on the left and right sides in between, both upper floors identical in floor plan. Tori's room lay in the back corner overlooking the garage, and from the door she could see a small bay window with a seat similar to what had been in the living area downstairs.

Pausing at the entrance and turning her back to her quarters, she could see the bathroom door along the wall a few paces to her right, the staircase that led to the third floor opening to her right in the center of the house, and a bedroom straight across from hers that belonged to Lindsey. She had remained silent for the tour, and her brow furrowed as she turned the full circle to take in the rest of her accommodations.

Shuffling inside, a spacious closet lay in the wall that the girls' rooms shared, and a second window on the back side of the house butted up to the other in the corner. A twin sized bed stuck out from the left hand wall as you entered, its nightstand effectively blocking access to the corner on the far side.

There stood a plain wooden rocking chair to the right of the door, and a tall dresser filled the corner on the other side of the closet. For a moment, Tori wondered if this had been arranged on purpose so that she would not have any corners to crouch into for sleeping, which was her normal routine.

Tossing her bag onto the bed, she stood for several minutes simply frowning at the space alone, as Sharon had disappeared. She hated it already. *This isn't fair.* She had given the Feds what they wanted, and she should be free, not trapped in some old wooden fire hazard with a bunch of strangers. *Fucking doctors*, she fumed to herself as she approached the window and glared down at the garage.

Brandon had gone out, and the wide door stood propped open while he rummaged around inside the structure. Tori's heart began to pound as she recognized the front wheel of a motorcycle peeking out from all the other visible junk. Turning quickly, her boots thumped loudly as she raced down the stairs, trying to make it before he closed it.

Catching her breath as she made her way up to the garage's entrance, the girl tried to hide her eagerness to get her hands on the bike. "Hi," she said as nonchalantly as she could muster. Brandon looked up, and his jaw dropped slightly in surprise to find her back outside so quickly. "This all your old stuff?" she asked while looking around.

Regaining his composure, he nodded, "Most of it."

Tori reached out to touch a few items, feigning curiosity, while inching her way closer to the half-buried treasure. She noted the layer of dust that covered most everything, and decided they must not visit the cramped space very often. Brandon watched her with curiosity as she finally reached her prize.

"This yours?" she asked, again trying to sound calm.

"Naw," he replied. "A tenant brought it in a few years ago, left it when he moved on." Tori began pulling items out of the way to have a better look. "Not sure what kind . . ." his voice trailed away, as she did not appear to be listening to him, having cleared a path and begun pushing it out into the evening sun.

"It's a '62 Honda Dream," she breathed, her eyes glistening as she ran her hand over the dents and rusted chrome. Tori had not known anything about motorcycles when the Dragons hit the road, but as Eddie's girl it became her job to learn. In five years, she had come to know them all, what they were, what they should look like, and how to make them purr. "Does it run?" She appeared eager, no longer able to conceal her enthusiasm.

"I don't think so," Brandon recalled with a shrug, "He parked it there and it's never been moved since, far as I know." Genuinely in awe of her behavior, he glanced up, noting the faces that stared down at them from the closest vantage points inside. "You know how to fix it?" His turn to try and sound nonchalant.

"Yeah," she exhaled loudly, "That I do." She ran her fingers across the seat and then down to the grease and dirt coated engine. Looking up from her squatted position, where she had been assessing the damage, her head cocked to one side, and a broad grin covered her glossy lips. "You mind if I work on it?"

"Knock yourself out," he replied, exposing a few teeth himself. "We should move some of this junk though, where you can push it in and out."

They shifted items to clear a path so she could get the bike parked with ease. The sun had dropped into setting position as the pair headed back into the house for dinner. Everyone gathering in the kitchen, they set the table and took their seats while Tori and Brandon washed up.

When they returned to the table, Tori realized dinner actually consisted of spaghetti with garlic bread. Her disappointment clear on her face, Richard piped up, "What's the matter? You don't like spaghetti? How could you *not* like spaghetti?"

Tori wrinkled her nose, "I don't eat this stuff... no bread or pasta. Meat, vegetables and fruits only, with water to drink."

"Oh," he blurted out, "The cave man diet."

She shot him a menacing look. *I've only been here an hour, and I'm already being insulted?*

Seeing her expression, he laughed and tried to explain. "No, no, that wasn't a jab. The proper name would be Paleo or Paleolithic diet. Called that because you eat like a caveman so to speak; all natural and nothing processed, like bread and pasta." Tori had never heard that her diet had a name, so she glowered at him in silence. Growing uncomfortable, he twirled his fork in his hand, "Anyways, that's what it's called. Sorry I offended you."

Deciding it wasn't worth any further discussion, Tori let the subject drop. Taking a small amount onto her plate, she gave it a try, but wasn't impressed. She picked out the meatballs and ate those, which were tasty, but not very filling. Excusing herself, she wanted to return to her room and put her things in a drawer; *and find where I'm going to sleep.*

Trudging up the stairs, she suddenly felt very weary. Removing her things from her bag, she organized them into the closet and one of the drawers in the tall dresser that blocked her corner. She slipped her journal into the narrowest drawer at the top, laying the pencil on top for easy access.

Placing her new running shoes, which Debra had taken her to purchase that morning, onto the floor in her closet, she thought about Debra and Eli. Wishing she could talk to them, she sat in the small window seat and looked at the sky outside. She had been to LA before, and knew there wouldn't be any stars for her to see. Peering down at the garage, she remembered the motorcycle, which brought her a small amount of comfort.

With a sigh, she decided it was time to go to sleep. Planning to get up early and run, she set the clock on the nightstand for 5:00 am. Only glancing down at the bed, she looked around at the room once more, disgusted that it had been arranged as it was, but disliking it was a moot point. She sank down against the wall and tried to sleep sitting up as best she could.

Music Maniac

With no corner to lean into, Tori found herself sprawled on the floor when the alarm went off. Stretching for several minutes beforehand, she got dressed in her new running pants and shoes and slipped downstairs as quietly as she could. Going out through the kitchen door, she noticed the coffee pot running. Inspecting it, she decided it had been placed on a timer, so someone would be up soon. Still being quiet, she exited the side door and headed down the steps of the porch.

Once she reached the street, Tori turned left and began to jog. Stopping what she judged to be the one mile mark, she began to stretch and do some squats. Continuing on, she ran another mile, then stopped again, noticing a playground.

Her heart pounded as she jogged over to the equipment and jumped to grab the bar. Finding it the perfect height, she did pull-ups and leg lifts, wishing there were some rings for muscle ups, as well. Dropping onto the ground, she did push-ups and then speed-skaters instead.

Working in sets of ten, she went ten rounds. Not really tired by that point, she glanced around, able to feel the time slipping away; she wanted to get back to the house before anyone missed her. Running at an easy jog, it was almost 6:00 am when she made it to the side entrance.

Bob almost dropped his coffee when she walked in, and she smiled at his look of terror at the back door unexpectedly opening. Apologizing, Tori explained that she worked out most every morning. Glad she had opted for the long spandex sleeves and leggings, she could feel him watching as she left the room. Having her scars exposed was simply not an option. Running up the stairs, she felt equally glad she had not washed off the previous day's makeup and hoped it had held up to the sweat.

Back in her room, she gathered her clothes and made her way to the bathroom next to her door. It turned out to be the three-quarter bath, but that suited her fine as she had never actually taken a tub bath in her life. Peeling off her damp workout clothes, she climbed into the shower and lathered quickly, using a tube of fruit scented gel that she found there.

The water felt good on her tingling skin, so she decided to wash her hair, as well. *It's pretty lucky there are only two girls here right now, as that gives Lindsey and I each a bathroom to ourselves.* After stepping out to dry off, she took her time putting on her special makeup, as she wanted it to be perfect. They were expecting her over to the music store later that morning to meet her new boss, and she wanted to make a good first impression if she could.

When dressed, she made her way back to her room and realized she did not have a specific place for her dirty clothes. She dropped them in front of the dresser on the floor, planning to ask about a laundry basket from Sharon when she saw her.

Checking her boots for creepy crawlies, she turned them upside down and slapped them a few times. Finding none, she pushed her feet inside. Her hair would be wet for a while, so she bent over and shook her hands through it roughly, then tossed it back with a swinging motion. She realized afterwards it might hit the ceiling when she did. *So strange having to worry about a roof over your head,* she sighed.

After she had finished primping, Tori trotted down the stairs. Reaching the bottom, she could smell bacon and eggs cooking, and hoped she would be able to have some, since dinner had been a little light. Inside the kitchen, Lindsey and Sharon were standing by the sink talking quietly until she entered the room. Giving her a warm greeting, both women were smiling.

Tori had made friends with Debra, so these two didn't scare her so badly. Heading over to the fridge to find a bottle of water, she gave them as warm a reply as she could muster.

Taking a cursory inventory, the large unit appeared packed with items, most of which Tori would never eat. Finding the water bottles, she grabbed one and let the door shut. "So, how does the food work around here anyways? Do I need to buy things I will eat for myself or do we have a community say?"

Sharon explained, "Everyone buys their own, and eats what they buy. However," she warned her with a small nod, "Leaving food out can result in someone else eating it. And we do try to do something for special occasions, like new arrivals and departures. That's why we made the spaghetti last night."

Tori nodded, figuring she wasn't getting any of the bacon and eggs. To her surprise, Lindsey spoke up and offered, "You want to share my breakfast? I mean, I'm sure you didn't bring any food in your suitcase."

Shaking her dark waves, she agreed she hadn't, not that she had any money for food either. She gladly accepted the offer, and the girls sat together for bacon and eggs with toast, which Tori passed on.

While they ate, Lindsey talked non-stop. She told her new friend where she was from, where she went to school, and why she was there. When their plates were clean, she finally drew a deep breath, and then asked, "So, what about you?"

Tori stared at her, wondering if the girl really wanted to

know and if she really wanted to tell. After a full minute of consideration, she simply replied, "My life hasn't been nearly as exciting as yours, I guess." Standing, she went over to the sink to wash her dishes and head out, as the clock read almost 10:00 am by then.

Today would be her first day at work, and she felt a little uneasy at the prospect of meeting more people, especially her boss. His being a former Fed caused her to hold a certain amount of distrust of him, even before she met him.

The agents who were on her committee had seemed honest and pleasant overall, but their holding her after she had fulfilled their agreement didn't sit well with the girl. *It's Dr. Bennet who had been the real problem,* she recalled, angry the Feds had sided with him.

Pulling out her map to the music store, she excused herself and exited through the side door. The store stood only ten blocks from the house, so she would be able to walk it pretty easily.

When she arrived at the address, Tori looked up to see *Music Maniac* in hot pink letters on the eave above the door. Inhaling deeply through her nostrils, she allowed the breath to escape through a relaxed jaw, then reached for the handle to go inside. The store dimly lit, she immediately removed her sunglasses to have a look around.

Placing them into her inner jacket pocket, she panned the room starting at the left, where rows upon rows of CD racks stood. The wall that held the door solid, it contained shelves running floor to ceiling from the entrance all the way to the corner.

The wall on the left of the room only had shelves up half way, and glass from the midline to the roof. There stood a second entrance made of two glass doors in the middle of it, which meant the building must sit on the corner. She hadn't noticed it before she came inside. The far wall had posters across it, with what appeared to be a small raised stage and three rows of benches in front, divided in half by a narrow walkway, like a cathedral.

On the right side of the sales floor, she could see the instrument section. A full rack of guitars hung on the wall behind a long glass L-shaped counter that continued all the way back around to the door. A six-foot sectional break in the counter held swinging doors for access to the back stock, as well as the entrances to get behind the glass cases.

A cash register sat mid counter, on the instrument side of the stock room, about halfway between the ends. She located the second one immediately to her right, on the side of the counter away from the exterior door. Tori made eye contact with a tall gentleman behind the closest one.

The man had been observing her since she walked in, and she gave him a small nod. He nodded back, and then commented, "You gotta be Tori." She could feel the hairs on her neck bristle at being recognized, but then of course he would be expecting her.

The shop owner had long black and grey hair that hung in tight waves, and a matching full beard and mustache that were several inches long. He wore a blue Hawaiian type shirt with large white flowers on it, and she could not help noticing his large round stomach; *if this is Terral Huffman, he has really let himself go.*

After the brief period of sizing each other up, Terral lifted his chin and spoke again, this time in Russian, "I hear you are quite a handful."

Tori nodded her agreement, and answered him in kind, "I can be."

Letting loose a loud belly laugh, he ambled to the opening in the glass to come around for a proper introduction. Offering his hand, he bellowed, "Good to meet you Tori. I'm Terral Huffman, but everyone calls me Terry."

The girl didn't return the smile or take his hand; rather she turned and walked away to inspect the guitars on the wall.

"You made these?" she indicated with a stiffened finger.

Terry felt a little put out she had snubbed his hearty welcome, but he didn't know her yet, either. Sidling over next to her, Tori noticed his limp and stiff left leg. He caught her staring at it, but shrugged it off, and made no reply. Exhaling a deep sigh, she went back to the Russian, as she had become aware of several young men were watching them from the entrance to the warehouse area.

"Look, Terry. I don't want to be here. And from what I understand, Godfry had to do some fancy finagling to get you to agree to it, so I'm guessing you feel the same way. So, let's cut to the chase. I will show up when I'm supposed to and do whatever you ask of me to the best of my ability. Don't ask me questions and don't ever touch me, and we'll get along fine."

She looked him dead in the eye as she spoke, and he knew he could take her at her word. "All right," he agreed, "then let's get to work."

Taking her on a tour, he showed her each of the sections out on the floor, Tori following behind him as he spoke. She removed her jacket and could hear laughter coming from the peanut gallery. She shot a nasty look in that direction, then continued to follow her boss, listening as he talked about the stage area, and moved towards the instrument counter.

Stopping to turn around while he explained, he saw her long sleeved tee and could not stop himself from commenting, "You know, you're gonna be hot working in that shirt." His choice of words sent the onlookers into hysterics, and she could see his cheeks turn a slightly deeper shade, while he pretended his comment had been purely innocent.

Tori's face like stone, she looked at the group

30

menacingly. Holding up her index finger she inquired, "Could you excuse me for just a sec?"

He nodded, somewhat leery of what would happen next, opting to wait and allow the interaction to unfold unimpeded.

Making her way over to the boys as they tried to stifle their laughter, she dropped her jacket on the end of the glass counter and moved a few steps closer. Standing with her feet apart, her left foot cocked ninety degrees to the right one, she pulled her hands up to her hips and cooed in a southern drawl, "Well, whatta fine mess we have here. You boys have names?"

One of them stood up straighter, grinning from ear to ear. "I'm Max," he announced proudly, shaking his long blond bangs out of his eyes. "This," he pointed, "Is Keith, and that's Derrick," he indicated the one leaning back in a chair against the corner of the doorframe.

Derrick busted out laughing, "What you even talkin' to her for, fool? Can't you tell she ain't from aroun' here?" he mocked her.

Tossing her ebony locks, the girl cracked a wide grin, and extended her hand, "Hiya Max; I'm Tori." His jaw dropped slightly in surprise, but he shook her extended appendage, and she held the accent beautifully. "Your frien's right; I'm ain't from aroun' here. Maybe you could take me t' dinner an' show me aroun' a bit?" She stepped closer to him and ran the back of her fingers down the front of his shirt.

His friends fell silent as he stammered for a moment, and then nodded his head heavily to agree.

Tori smiled again, "Great. I'll see ya after work then." Patting his chest with the palm of her hand, she turned on her heel and picked up her jacket. She rejoined Terry with a sly smile, swaying her hips as she moved.

"You know he's just a kid," Terry stated quietly when she was back in ear shot.

31

Tori gave him a half grin, "I'm only fifteen, myself."

Terry barked a sharp laugh while shaking his head. "I don't know who's the bigger fool; the guy who came up with that bullshit, or the ones who bought it." Not wanting to dig any deeper into what his old friend might be up to, he let the subject go and continued the tour while Tori listened attentively.

The store closes at 8:00 pm each night, so they began straightening up about 7:30. Max made his way closer to Tori as they worked the racks and cleaned all of the glass. "Are you really going to go have dinner with me after work?" he asked in a timid voice.

Giving him a sideways look, Tori's lips curled into a small smile, "Only if you want to."

His eyes bright, he grinned and increased his arm speed in an effort to finish early and be off on their date. Noticing Terry watching her, she made her way over to him, trying to look natural.

"Relax," she told him in a patronizing voice, "I'm not going to hurt him, I swear." She held up her right hand as a solemn oath.

Terry didn't look convinced, but said nothing more about it. When the clock above the swinging doors read five to close, Terry began setting up the registers, and then went to lock the doors. When he came back, he motioned Tori over, "I want to show you how to shut down the drawers."

She commented mockingly, "I'm somewhat surprised you would trust me with your money so soon."

"Yeah, well, from what I hear, you're a murderer, not a thief," he replied with a smug grin.

His words stung her, and he could see her deflate as she murmured, "Well, that's true."

She watched obediently as he showed her what to do on the first machine, and then asked her to repeat the process for him on the second. She didn't miss a step, and he smiled at her genuinely. She seemed dispirited after his comment, and he regretted having made it. "Come in at eight in the morning, I'll show you how to open," he said as he headed to the office in the back.

Max walked up to her, smiling warmly, but her mood had been lost, and she could not muster one for him in return. Sensing her unhappiness, he reached out and entwined his fingers with hers, soothing, "It's your first day. Don't sweat it." Tori appreciated the kind words, and gave his digits a small squeeze as they strolled out the door.

Old Habits

The pair walked along the sidewalk, swinging their still connected hands to some slow, unheard melody. Reaching the small diner that stood four blocks down from the double doors of the shop, Max held the entrance for her as she made her way inside.

Mmm, a gentleman, she thought to herself, realizing she had not seen many of those in her lifetime. Sliding into a round booth in the corner, Tori appreciated being able to see the expanse of the room, as she still harbored a deep distrust of people. Max scooted around next to her comfortably, giving her a sheepish smile of excitement. He appeared clearly pleased she seemed interested in him.

The waitress made her way over to their table, and Max smiled at Tori as he asked what she wanted. Shrugging, she replied, "Something with meat and vegetables." The waitress nodded, putting pot roast on the ticket, while Max ordered a cheeseburger and French fries. Tori wrinkled her nose at his choice, which made him laugh and finally brought a small smile to her lips.

"So, what's your story?" he asked, folding his arms on the table to lean on when they were alone.

Tori shook her head, too tired of her own misery to even begin to explain. "I got nothing," she stated after a long pause, her expression a blank stare, "I'd rather hear about you."

At her request, Max began to talk about his life, his

dreams, and whatever popped into his head. Eventually their meal arrived, and they ate with little conversation, as she felt terribly grateful for the first good meal she had had since her arrival.

When he finished, the boy began to talk about himself again, and Tori sat half listening while she watched him. She noticed that he had bright green eyes, when she could see them through his shaggy bangs. She decided she liked the way the hairs brushed his pointy nose and had him swooshing them out of the way with his fingers on occasion. She especially liked his smooth lips, and noticed the way one side curved more than the other when he smiled, causing a deep dimple in his left cheek.

The sun had set outside, and she could feel the night closing in around them. While she considered these things, she unexpectedly leaned forward and kissed him, her left hand moving up to catch his neck and hold him in place while she did so.

Immediately, she felt her heart begin to pound with excitement, and an aching need sprang up inside her. Max, being young and eager, kissed her back, his hands instantly roaming beneath her jacket, searching for her soft round curves.

His left hand slid up to caress her right breast, his thumb moving back and forth across the point. Forgetting they were still sitting in a public place, the two allowed their hands to wander freely, and Tori heard herself moan with anticipation.

Moments later, she broke off the kiss, Terry's voice jumping to the front of her mind, screaming loudly. Grabbing his probing fingers with her right hand, she became keenly aware of the moistness forming in her warm folds of flesh and the ache between her thighs. Licking her lips anxiously, she slid back on the seat to put some inches between them, panting as she tried desperately to put on the breaks.

"What's the matter?" his voice cracked, obviously upset.

Glancing back at him as she slithered on around to the left and stood up, she stammered, "It's not your fault. It's mine. I should never have come here. I'm sorry." She fled before he could pursue her, turning at the corner and heading for home. Feeling like shit every step of the way, her thoughts churned; *he's just a kid—what the hell were you thinking?*

She kept walking as fast as she could without actually breaking out into a run. When she reached the music store, she hung a left and kept moving. *Five blocks to go, you can get there;* Tori gave herself a pep talk at a red light while she waited to cross.

Swinging her gaze absently down the road, she saw a liquor store on the next corner, and her pounding heart stopped dead for an instant. Breathing heavily, the light changed to green for her, but she didn't even notice, her mind racing in another direction.

Whisked into the past, Tori felt herself sitting in a chair, facing a table in the center of the bush camp, in Brazil. That had been her home, where she had grown up. A place she had shared with Eli and the committee because she had to, but she had no intention of anyone else ever finding out about it, or any of the other ugly things in her past.

She wet her lips as she stared down the busy street. *I don't even have any money;* she realized, then countered the thought with a frown, *you don't need that shit, get your ass home at a reasonable hour!* Swinging her focus back to the light, it had cycled to red again. *Damn it.* The cool night breeze made the wetness inside her jeans uncomfortable as she stood waiting, tortured by her actions and her desire for what lay next to her, a few doors down.

Tori stood facing the way she wanted to walk, but in the fresh darkness, the lights of the store to her right burned in her mind. She could feel herself in that chair, with David Long sitting beside her and coaching her on how to down the shots.

She licked her lips again nervously and looking down at her hands noticed they had begun to tremble. Clenching them into fists repeatedly, she crossed on the green light and walked as quickly as she could towards the tall brown haven. *I don't need that shit;* she repeated to herself as she marched. *I only drank to do what I had to do. It's just an old habit; it'll pass.*

Hitting the back door and practically bolting inside, she froze in her tracks as she entered the kitchen. The clock above the doorway into the hall read 10:30; *I'm not late, thank God!*

Sharon stood at the coffee pot, returning the carafe to its hotplate. "Hi," she said in an upbeat tone. "We were afraid you might have gotten lost," dropping a brief pause; "We thought your shift ended at eight. Would you like some coffee?"

"It did," Tori stammered, trying to keep her cool. "I had dinner with one of the guys from the shop." *See...that wasn't so bad.* She ran her fingers through her hair while considering a cup of java. She didn't drink coffee, or anything other than water or liquor for that matter, very often.

Still standing just inside the doorway, she rationalized she really hadn't done anything wrong. *So I kissed the guy and let him cop a feel, so what? Nothing really bad happened.* She raised her chin defiantly, shoving her hands into her pockets to hide the tremor that would give her away. "Anyways, I think I'll head up to bed. Goodnight." She darted for the door and went up the stairs, her boots loud on the wooden case.

Watching her go, Sharon had a heavy feeling in the pit of

her stomach. *It's Tori's second night here, and already she's struggling.* Taking a sip of her coffee, she moved to join her husband at the table, who had been watching quietly as the events unfolded before him.

"Did you see it?" he asked as she sat down.

"Yeah, I saw it," she replied with a knowing look. Sharon, a recovering alcoholic, had been sober for ten years. But deep down, she knew the ache of the people who pass through her home, and understood their pain.

Meanwhile, Tori made it to her bedroom door, closing it loudly behind her. She stood for several minutes in the center of her room panting, hands still buried in her jacket.

Thinking about Paul, she recalled how he had followed her around with a bottle of rum the first night she drank herself into a stupor and let the Dragons have her body to do with as they pleased. So much time had passed, but she could still feel the cold wood of the table against her naked skin as they fucked her. Closing her eyes, she allowed the memory to progress, surrounding her, and she could hear the trees as they moved in the breeze.

Eddie had been on the ground leaning against the cabin, when Tori straddled him, sitting on his lap and making her move. She had asked, *"Can I take my clothes off now?"* and his hands had been on her in an instant.

She could feel his fingers as they worked their way back and forth across her back, then pulling her forward in an arch that pushed her breasts out further in front of her. He had cupped her right breast and toyed with it through the cloth. He nuzzled her cheek and whispered loudly, *"Oh yeah, baby girl, you should most definitely...take them off."* She could tell it pleased him that she wanted to be his.

Tori rose and silently removed her boots, then her pants and shirt. The onlookers had once again lain themselves out around the firelight to watch, but this night would be different. This night, she wanted to be a willing participant, and she had no choice but to play the part. Never again would they take her by force; not if she could help it.

She removed her bra and panties and stood completely naked before the man who owned her. He reached up, running his fingers lightly across the bandage that covered her healing wound. He sneered as he did so, knowing the brand meant the others and any man who was with her knew whom she belonged to.

He opened his pants and instructed her to get on her knees. Kneeling on the ground before him, she wasn't sure how to please him, having only touched Henry the one time a few short nights before. He guided her head with his hand as she took him in her mouth, and it made her gag as he forced his hardened organ into her throat.

Tori managed to hold back the urge to vomit, and did her best to please him. After a few minutes, he used her hair to pull her to her feet, and then walked her over to the table where the tube of gel awaited.

Turning her to face the table, he pushed her down so that her belly lay flat against the cold hard wood. His fingers were rough as he used the gel to smooth his path. She began to pant in ragged breaths as she realized he did not intend to take her as he should have, opting for the position that hurt her so badly. She gripped the edges of the table, refusing to cry as he made his way inside, and she fought to control her breathing and hold her façade in place.

He slapped against her for several minutes, and Tori could feel her legs twitch from their awkward dangling position. He grasped the skin along her ribs tightly between his fingers and palms, his breath loud as his moans and grunts rose to their final peek, and then he stood still, pulsing inside her.

Leaning over her naked back, he rested on top of her so

that he could breathe against her neck and whisper in her ear. He stroked her hair as he exhaled, *"So good, baby girl."* Her left cheek pressed against the table, she stared blankly into the night, unwilling to respond.

Finished with her, he slid himself out, and walked away to allow the others to take what they wanted. Tori didn't move or struggle against them, only allowing herself to grip the edges of the table and breathe to relax and accept them being inside her. She did not bother to keep track of who or how many, as it didn't matter. That was her life; that was her place, her job in the darkness.

Back in her room in the halfway house, Tori stood still for a moment longer as the memory faded back into the recesses of her mind. Pulling off her jacket, she tossed it onto the rocking chair beside the door. Stripping down, she put her clothes onto the laundry pile, thinking it would be a waste to wash them yet, as she had only worn them for a day. She frequently wore the same set for a week out on the road.

Putting on her sleep shorts and tee, she looked around the room in disgust. They had blocked every single corner with furniture. Leaning into the closet, she surveyed the tiny space.

A built in shelving unit ran all along the back wall that was about a foot deep. Both sides held two hanging bars that were three foot long, with a shelf halfway up, above the lower rod. Kneeling down, she slid under the bar to the right of the door facing out into the bedroom and worked her right shoulder into the corner.

It felt odd, actually sitting in the closet, gripping the doorframe as she tried to breathe calmly. Sleep didn't come easy that night, so she had time to reflect on her day and formulate a plan.

First off, I will be respectful of Terry. Whatever his reasons for allowing her to work for him, she was there now and needed the job and all it had to offer.

Secondly, I need to stay the hell away from those boys. Her *no touch policy* would need to be strictly enforced, as Max had already proven to be more than willing to go for a romp if she ever wanted one, which she didn't.

Third, under no circumstances will I allow myself a drink or even a taste of alcohol. No matter what, it would be essential that she stay sober and not fuck things up. Deep down, Tori knew she could do this; *I'm smart and strong after all, and I have survived much worse than this.*

Her mind drifting to Eli, she became riddled with guilt about her behavior that night, for his sake. She felt ashamed she had let another man touch her so soon after their night together and also glad he would never find out she had done so.

Her feelings for Eli had grown strong during the time they had spent together, and although they really didn't have much in common, she knew their future together would be a good one. As her mind began to wind down, Tori finally fell asleep in the darkness of the closet, the comforting coolness of the wall pressing against her face.

Get a Routine

Tori awoke when her alarm went off at 5:00 am, leaning into her corner in the closet. She had slept only marginally better than the first night, still upset with herself and her actions the day before. Dressing for her run and workout, she shuddered to think what might have happened if they had been someplace more private. The thought excited her for a moment, and she quickly admonished herself; *you can bury that idea for good, and you're gonna avoid that situation all together.*

Heading down the stairs and out the side door, she took the same path she had the day before, this time moving out onto the grass and doing some other exercises to vary her routine. She pushed herself hard, almost as a punishment for her misdeeds, doing twelve sets of twelve before she turned back to the house.

Bob didn't react this time when she opened the door, only lifting his head from his newspaper long enough to wish her a good morning. Tori answered likewise as she exited through the far door, eager for her shower.

A few minutes later, she stood beneath the cascade of warm water. Allowing it to soak her thoroughly, she used the peach scented gel to lather her skin and relax her exhausted muscles. She dressed in haste and put on her makeup quickly, pleased she got better at it each time she did so.

Finally, she put on a fresh pair of jeans and another long sleeved white tee; finally she checked her boots and pulled those on, as well. She didn't stop for breakfast this morning, exiting the house straight away. She made her way over to the garage and pulled on the handle. It wasn't locked and swung open with ease.

In the early gray light of dawn, she could barely see the machine, but it gave her enough to get a mental picture and an idea of some of the work that needed to be done. Closing the door tightly, Tori hoped focusing on the bike would give her something to think about that did not involve sex or drugs, both of which she wanted desperately to avoid.

Deciding she had a few minutes, she went back inside, where Bob had finished his morning routine and was about to go back upstairs. Noticing her looking around the kitchen, he pointed to the fridge, "Grab some of my fruit if you like. It's in the bottom drawer with my name on it." He smiled as he spoke, and she tried to respond with one of her own, but felt exposed, as if everyone in the house could read her dirty thoughts and judged her for her stupidity.

Pulling out an orange and two plums, she snagged a bottle of water and sat at the table a few minutes munching on them. The clock read 7:15 and she did not want to be late. Taking the bottle with her, she made her trek to the store at a brisk pace.

Reaching the light at the halfway point, Tori kept her eyes straight ahead, not even allowing herself to look at her nemesis that now stood on her left. When the light turned green, she moved ahead swiftly and arrived at the store with plenty of time to spare.

Seeming to be the first one there, she checked both doors to find them locked, and no one answered when she knocked. Leaning with her back against the wall alongside the single door, she propped her foot up next to her knee, the sole pressing against the concrete partition, her hands shoved in her pockets.

A few minutes later, Terry drove up and parked down the block. He could see her relaxed position as he moved to exit the vehicle, and grinned to himself. Thinking back, he wasn't sure exactly what had made him agree to his old friend's request. *It's true*, he recalled; *it had taken a fair amount of convincing to sell me on the idea.*

Huffman had been a career man in the agency, with no family to speak of and no friends outside of it for many years. He had been involved in bringing down his share of bad guys, and although he still felt good about his job, he had been tired by the time he called it quits. Tired of the pain and misery humans could cause one another.

In the end, that's what had sold him on allowing her there. *That girl's seen more than her share of pain and misery; what I hope to give her most is some tools she can use to build a real future for herself.* He reminded himself of his motives as he approached her, hoping to convey his feelings of good will.

Smiling warmly as he drew close, he spoke in a friendly tone, "Well, nice to see you so bright and early."

Tori managed a small grimace, not quite able to hold his eyes, allowing hers to dart away before looking at the ground. She could feel the stab of guilt, and she wondered if he knew about Max and what she had allowed to happen. She followed him inside without speaking, suddenly glad to be there, where she might be able to get a routine in her life.

Terry did not question her odd behavior. Instead, he got right to work, explaining his short list of lessons for the day, "I'm going to teach you how to open the store, count the previous day's sales, and prepare the deposit."

"I still don't understand why you want me to do this," she told him bitterly. "I just got here, and I'm sure one of those other guys would be much better suited."

Terry only grinned at her observation, not bothering to

reply. Godfry had called the girl a genius. *"But she doesn't know it, so you might keep it to yourself,"* his friend had advised. *She obviously undervalues herself,* he assessed. He would have to work on helping her build her confidence and self-esteem, which would be a long and slow process.

Pulling out the money from the night before, he showed her how to count each till and subtract the starting cash each register begins the day with. He then showed her how to pull the sales reports and reconcile the two. Finally, they made out the deposit slip, which they placed in a zippered bag with the cash for deposit, and locked it in the safe to be taken to the bank later in the day. Taking the starting funds, he walked her out to the floor to show her how to open the registers.

Tori was sharp, exactly as Godfry had promised, picking up on the process with relative ease. The pair opened both registers, and then made a quick sweep of the store to be sure everything would be ready for opening. At 10:00 am, Derrick and Max arrived, being the morning crew for the day.

Max stared at her coldly, obviously a bit put out at the way she had left him the night before. Derrick laughed, and as he walked behind her towards the back of the store, he leaned over and uttered a single word; "Tease."

So, Max had seen fit to share the events with his friend. That's fine, Tori consoled herself; *that will make it easier not to repeat.*

The two young men were put to work on the front, cleaning and running the registers, and Terry led Tori to the back to finish showing her the store's overall routine. The back divided into two basic sections, he pointed out that the left contained the small office and a receiving area where a large overhead door stood for unloading trucks. On the right stood a workshop of sorts, where he did, in fact, build the guitars that he sold.

45

Giving her a quick overview of the process, he explained that after he left the agency, he felt like a broken man, who needed something to do with his hands. "So, I learned to build guitars. It has helped me cope and feel useful in my retirement."

He smiled at her, and Tori felt very appreciative of his efforts. She noticed that his eyes were blue, like hers, and found herself staring into them for a few moments as she considered exactly what it might have been he was coping with.

"How long were you with the agency?" she asked in a quiet voice.

Nodding his head, he responded in a low tone, "Twenty five years."

Breaking their eye contact, Tori looked around at the wooden counters strewn with tools and guitar parts, thinking to herself, *it must be nice to have a purpose; something to do that's for a good reason or cause.* Remembering the bike parked in the garage, she felt the urge to go look for parts.

Turning abruptly, he bade her to follow him over to the office, where he opened the safe and handed her an envelope. "I thought you could use an advance," he stated calmly, "Since you're just starting out."

Tori peeked into the white pouch and counted three $100 bills. It gave her stomach a funny twinge that he gave her money, and she looked at his face for a moment, not sure what to do or say next.

Noting her confusion, he smiled and clarified, "It's just an advance. Take it and get what you need, and I'll deduct it from your paycheck, let's say fifty dollar installments for six checks."

Looking down at the cash again, she managed a small smile and thanked him quietly. His kindness touched her, and Tori realized for the first time that caring people were not such a rarity after all. Eli and Debra had only been the start of all the people she would meet in her life; people who would help her on her journey. Meeting his warm blue eyes, she grinned, and spoke with more confidence, "Really, thank you very much. I will do my best to deserve it."

"You already deserve it," he laughed as he gave her a quick slap on the shoulder, "Now, go take the rest of the day off, get what you need to make yourself at home in your new life."

Tori nodded, slipped the envelope into her jacket pocket and headed towards the front. Making her way across the sales floor, she could see the two boys snickering at her as she exited, but she wasn't going to let them bother her. She had too many other things to worry about.

Making a Way

Tori left the shop and returned to the house straightaway. Once inside, she located Brandon in his office, shuffling through a pile of papers. Knocking lightly on the open door, she got his attention. Giving him a shy smile, she requested, "Can I come in? I have a few questions, if you have the time to help me." He immediately shoved the stack back into the plastic tray and waved her into the room, pleased at the surprise visit.

Taking a seat in the folding chair across from him, she explained that Terry had given her some cash, and she faced the issue of never having handled money on her own before. She had $300 in her pocket, and she realized if he were going to be taking out $50 a week to pay it back, she was going to need some skills to go about it the right way.

"Let me make a few calls," he told her patiently, so Tori moved over into the living area while she waited. Walking around the room, looking at the simple decorations, her mind drifted away, and she recalled what the Dragons had taught her about money.

It had been a cold evening in the fall, and the group had stopped over in a medium sized town in Indiana. They were at a small local dive with a loud jukebox and cheap liquor. Some of the guys were playing pool, and Tori, already drunk, busied herself giving head in the back corner.

A man came in to see Eddie, and they sat at a table alone for about half an hour talking business. When it came time to

48

close up, Eddie paid the barkeep to let them stay the night, telling him they would be gone by first light, and they had fucked her on the pool table after he left.

The next day, they didn't leave town, which meant Eddie had picked up some work from the guy the night before. The Dragons messed around for the day, working on their bikes, doing laundry and what have you.

As night fell, Eddie handed Tori a picture of a woman, with an address to a shoe store at the bottom and 10:00 pm beside the word *front* written on the side. His only command, "Take care of this."

She shoved it in her pocket, understanding without question what he meant. Getting on the back of Bill Rightmer's bike, they rode across town, and he dropped her off a few blocks away. Tori made her way over the few streets, taking up a location where she could monitor the entrance to the store.

Pulling out the picture, she studied it carefully. A thin middle aged woman, she had dark hair and brown eyes. Her clothes were plain, a simple smile on her face. Tori shoved the picture back into her pocket and waited.

A short while later, the woman came out the glass door of the building and began to walk towards her. After the girl passed where she leaned against a brick wall, Tori fell into step about ten paces behind her.

They walked for about three blocks, Tori maintaining her distance, keeping her steps in time with the woman's, who did not even seem aware of being followed. Turning down a narrower side street, she adjusted her purse strap on her shoulder, obviously tense about either this stretch of her journey or perhaps the upcoming route.

Tori widened her steps and quickened her pace, while continuing to mask her own steps with the loud clickety-click that the woman's heels made as they struck the concrete.

Turning again, the woman entered a dark alley, and Tori caught up just after the shadows had fully engulfed her.

Taking her from behind with her left hand, she clamped down hard over the woman's mouth to stifle any scream that might escape. In the same motion, the blade shot out the end of her knife with a loud pop, and Tori's right hand brought it up and slit her throat in a single fluid pull, letting her body fall to the ground as she unlaced the purse off her arm and swung it over her own.

Bending over, Tori cleaned the blade of her knife on the back of the woman's clothing with a few quick swipes, snapped it shut and retraced her steps, out of the alley. Strolling the few blocks over, she met up with Bill at their rally point.

The job had paid $15K and had taken less than an hour to carry out. That's what the Dragons had taught her about money. If you were good, the money came easy, and so they never had a shortage of cash on the road. The Feds confiscated over $100K that had been found in the farmhouse and on their bikes after they swept the scene the day Tori and the rest of the Dragons were found. Only carry around cash, the bulk of their funds remained secretly tucked away in various locations across the country for safe keeping.

Brandon called to her from the doorway, interrupting her thoughts, and she turned to rejoin him in the office. He had called Terry to confirm what she would be earning in the way of income, and felt somewhat surprised at the salary she would be receiving, fairly certain it was more than he paid his other employees. But then again, Terry owned the business, so he could pay her whatever he wanted.

Taking their seats, Brandon went over how taxes worked and what would be deducted from her gross income. Using the adding machine, he showed her how to calculate her withholdings and what her net income would be.

Tori stared at the amount in disbelief. *No wonder the Dragons chose a life of crime,* she thought as she glared at the paltry sum. She sat blinking at it as if it might change, and Brandon chuckled at her response.

"Don't worry," he reassured her. "It's more than enough. Now, let me show you how to make a budget."

The pair sat for over an hour, yellow legal pad in hand, as he showed her what normal expenses would look like and how much to allot for each. By the end, she had a plan for handling her money, which included putting a small amount each week into savings and having some to spend on parts for repairing the motorcycle.

After they had her finances in order, Brandon gave her directions to a supermarket within walking distance. She thanked him whole-heartedly and headed out into the afternoon sun.

Hiking at a steady pace, Tori went over the conversation and the advice Brandon had given her about making her way in the world, and having a healthy and stable life. By the time she reached the store, her mind had begun to find doubt in his words that the money would be enough. She had begun to consider how she could come up with a little extra cash to supplement her meager income.

Briefly, she deliberated the possibility she could lift a small amount from the store, certain that Terry would never miss it. Almost immediately, she dismissed the thought as she remembered his biting words, *"You're a murderer, not a thief."* Besides, Tori appreciated his efforts to help her and did not want to hurt him in return.

Of course, with no real solution at the moment, she would simply have to keep an eye out and be ready for any opportunities that presented themselves along the way where she could make a quick and quiet buck.

Entering the supermarket, Tori turned to the left and

made her way to the far end. Working her way across, she explored every aisle while pushing a large empty cart in front of her. She chose a nice smelling shampoo and conditioner for her hair, and selected shave gel and razors for her legs and pits.

She had a couple of bottles of the special creamy makeup that Debra had helped her find and a phone number to order more of it when her supply ran out. However, she decided to purchase some new colors of the powder that she smoothed on her eyelids and a couple of new shades of gloss for her lips.

Picking out the personal items, her mind drifted to Eli, and how he had told her she was beautiful, even without the makeup. Tori felt overcome with feelings of shame at what she had been considering on her journey to the store. Eli would be mortified if he knew what she had been thinking, and she had again let him down.

She could picture him at that moment, sitting in his barren apartment alone, pining for her return. Making her way through the aisles of processed foods she would never touch, she made a promise to herself; *I'm going to do a good job at getting better, and Eli will be waiting for me when I'm finally free.*

Eventually reaching the opposite end of the store from where she started, Tori entered an open expanse of fruit and vegetable tables, and she could feel her spirits lift at the sight of them. Picking her way through, she chose small bags of carrots and broccoli, tiny red potatoes, fixings for a salad, and five or six kinds of fruit, including the small red cherries she loved so much. Filling her basket, she began to hum lightly as she dreamed about being back in Chicago with Eli and shopping with him for more tasty dinners that they would share.

Moving along the back of the store, Tori found the meat

counter and chose a few steaks and a package of fish. Noting how expensive the meats were, she considered being faithful to her new ideals would be a challenge. Peering at the large clock over the front doors, she realized she needed to hurry if she wanted to have a meal. She had an AA meeting that night, and although she felt displeased about it, she had promised herself to stay on the straight and narrow path being laid before her, and she intended to do exactly that.

No Need for Help

Tori made it back to the house in time to prepare a small dinner of fish and vegetables, and had a bowl of naturally sweet fruit for dessert. She had not purchased any water since it would have been heavy to carry, so she wrote herself a note to ask Sharon about how she could get water efficiently. She also intended to ask about the laundry basket she needed. While she sat looking at her short list of things to do, Jonathon came in from upstairs and inquired if she were ready to go.

Looking up at him from her seat at the dining table, her mind went blank as to where they were going. Seeing her vacant expression, he explained that he would be going to the AA meeting with her, as he attended them weekly, as well.

Reluctantly, Tori stood, and they made their way out the door. Walking beside him, she noted that he fell a bit on the short side, like Eli, and she could see clearly over his head. A bit pudgy, she briefly considered his diet and the amount of food he consumed, and understood why.

The two walked in silence, and upon reaching the small brick building where the meetings were held, she shuffled away from him and chose a cozy corner to stand in and watch. A social creature, Jon eagerly greeted other attendees with high fives and vigorous handshaking.

Tori felt almost certain he knew everyone in the room, and a pang of envy stabbed her heart. Not that she wanted to be friends with these people, *God no*. She was jealous that he could be so open, so alive and happy to share in conversation and laughter without a second thought.

Drawing close to meeting time, she avoided sitting beside him and chose a chair at the end of a row close to the door, in case she wanted to ditch out early. Various people took the podium to speak, and they always began by giving their name and stating that they were an alcoholic.

Tori scoffed at them in her heart, telling herself they were fools. A strong and intelligent woman, she sure as hell had no need for help, not from them or from anyone. *Besides, I'm not really an alcoholic anyways. It's already been two months since I've had a drink, and I'm doing fine.*

The meeting only lasted an hour, but it seemed an eternity. When it finally ended, she jumped to her feet, intending to bolt out the door. Before she reached it, Jon grabbed her by the arm, "Hey, a group of us are heading over to a diner for coffee and apple pie. You should join us, make some friends." He smiled, hoping she would come along.

Tori pulled her arm away with an exaggerated jerk, spitting out, "No, thanks!" as she made a break for it. She practically ran back to the house, dropping on the swing at the end of the porch when she arrived.

Leaning forward, she put her elbows on her knees and her face into her hands, sitting hunched over to catch her breath. Once she felt rested, she leaned back into the swing. The sunset allowed the darkness to slowly surround her. Her feet flat on the wood of the porch, she pushed the swing lightly and allowed herself to enjoy the evening quiet. In her old life, it would be time to start hitting a few shots and removing her clothes.

With the Dragons, Tori had served as the nightly entertainment; her job as Tony had once put it, and she accepted her position within the group without protest. She had put up a fight in the beginning, and still had the scars to prove it. She learned quickly that letting them have what they wanted gave her an advantage, as her clothes stayed cleaner, and she hurt far less when they were finished with her.

The only one who really tortured her had been Red, Eddie's brother. He liked to do things to her that were especially brutal when he fucked her, and Tori learned to accept the pain as part of the process. In the end, he got what he had coming to him. The girl sneered evilly as she recalled what she had done to him in the farmhouse before bludgeoning him to death without remorse.

While she sat in the sway of the swing, she thought about how she had slowly come to accept her position within the Dragons. For as long as Henry had been around, she had been almost content as the slut of the group, although he was not permitted to partake of her.

Henry had been her first, the only man she had chosen, more or less. She allowed her mind to retrace their night together as she sat in the warm evening air rocking gently, much like the night they had held each other all those years ago.

Eventually, Tori stood and made her way into the house and up the stairs to her room. She felt overly tired, and undressed slowly, donning her sleeping attire and crawling into her corner in the closet to sleep. The alarm went off at 5:00 am as usual, and her day began again.

She fell into a pattern of similar routine for a couple of weeks, early to rise, exercise and then work. She returned home in the late afternoons or evenings to make her dinner, and found time to work on the motorcycle a few times, as well.

By the end of the third week, Tori spoke to no one she didn't have to, and kept to herself in a type of brooding silence. She hated her life there and simply went through the motions, trying to hang on. She dreamt of being free to return to Chicago and going back to Eli, who waited for her.

Walking home one afternoon at the end of the fourth week, she had an idea that lifted her spirits. *I should call him.* He wasn't able to visit her, but the sound of his voice would surely give her strength to make it through.

Rushing back to the house, the girl realized she had never gotten any contact information from him, but she felt confident she would be able to reach him through the federal offices where he worked. They would be able to forward her call, and she could hear his voice.

Considering how to get the number, she slipped into the house quietly, trying to avoid being seen or heard. Making her way down the hall, she peeked into the living room and finding it empty, she exhaled a sigh of relief. Turning towards the office, the door stood open, with the chair on the far side of the desk vacant as well.

Stepping across the hall with purpose, Tori flipped through the Rolodex that sat on the desk, searching the sections for the right entry. Finally finding it, she removed the card, noting its location so she could return it later. With a firm tug to free it from the tabs, she shoved it in her pocket and flipped the file back to the front. Turning and heading back out of the house, she made her way to the supermarket almost in a dead run.

Two payphones stood in front of the store. The devices are extremely rare these days, but at least there are still enough people using them to have a few left around. Dropping in a handful of coins, she pulled out the card and typed in the number.

Bouncing at her knees out of nervous excitement, she licked her lips as the phone began to ring. Finally, a woman's voice answered the line, "Federal Bureau of Investigation, Chicago office, how may I direct your call?"

Tori stammered slightly as she asked, "Can I please

speak to Special Agent Eli Founder?" and a smile flitted across her features as she spoke his name.

After a brief pause, the woman replied, "I'm sorry; Agent Founder is no longer assigned to this office."

Tori's heart stopped cold. Unable to breathe, she stuttered, "What happened? I've only been gone a few weeks," her mind spinning, she pled in desperation, "Where is he now? How can I contact him? Please, give me the new number."

"I'm sorry," the woman stated again, "I cannot give you that information."

Tori stood frozen, wondering what in the hell happened. Quickly, she insisted, "Listen, it's very important that I speak to Eli."

She was met with equally strong resistance from the other end of the line. "I'm not at liberty to discuss any agent's assignment with you."

"Who can I speak to then? Please, put me through to Debra Paisley." Tori grasped for straws, her heart pounding wildly inside her rib cage. Upon hearing Debra could not be reached either, she realized her endeavor had turned up fruitless; no one in Chicago who could help her.

Tori silently hung up the phone and stood for a moment, staring blankly at the brick wall in front of her. *Eli is gone. Eli is gone!* The thoughts ran into chaos in her brain, and she could feel the deep ache in her chest. She had felt this pain before, the day Henry had died. The minutes ticked by as she stood with her hand still pulling down on the receiver as it hung in its cradle, her mind lost in a conundrum of thoughts and emotions.

Finally, she released her grip on the device and slowly trudged away from the storefront. Making her way along the streets, she found the corner that held a large plain building with a glass front, four blocks east and five blocks south of the shop.

Winding a path among the rows of bottles, she could feel the clerk watching her as she found the containers of vodka. Taking her time, as if she knew exactly what kind she wanted, she read the labels to herself.

There are many brands and flavors of the vile liquid, and Tori would choose her favorite. She had drunk many a bottle of liquor over the years. He felt like an old friend, always ready to take her in and comfort her when the world around her became bleak. Selecting a fifth of Smirnoff Silver, she made her way to the counter, placing her product on it with a thud.

The man behind the wooden expanse looked down at the glass container, then back up at her face like carved stone. "Got any ID?" his tone came out flat, and not really a question.

Tori shifted her gaze around the deserted store and licked her upper lip tensely. "How about Ulysses S. Grant?" she asked, giving him a hint of a smile.

His grin broad, he replied, "I like Ben Franklin better."

While Tori pulled her wallet out of her back pocket, he placed the bottle in a plain brown bag. She handed him a $100 bill, grabbed the bottle through the sack and headed out the front door.

Making her way to the back, she walked a couple of blocks down the alley before choosing a spot, sinking to the ground beside a dumpster. Opening the bottle, she put the glass to her lips and chugged a third of the liquid, enjoying the burn in her throat as it went down.

Breathing heavily for several minutes, she blinked back the tears that were collecting in her crystal blue eyes. Lifting the bottle again, she finished it off with ease, then stood, smashing it against the wall as she headed home, hoping she would make it before the darkness overtook her.

No Place Like Home

Tori could feel the tingle in her lip as she chewed it while climbing the steps of the veranda. Entering through the back door, she hoped she didn't stagger. A few of her roommates were in the kitchen putting together their dinner, and Lindsey seemed happy to see her.

Over the past few weeks, the girl had sat with her several times for long chats that reminded Tori of the days she had spent with Eli when she first awoke in the hospital. Lins would talk about anything and everything, and Tori would listen in silence, taking it all in. The thought of the similarity made her weary with grief as she made her way through the kitchen door and into the hall, announcing loudly she didn't feel well and would be going to bed early.

Enrique Dominguez, brand new to the house, had arrived only three days before. When he first moved in, he had not seemed impressed with the taller of the females; although beautiful, she had an unhappy disposition and sullen attitude.

Enrique came into the house under court order, and although he didn't want any trouble, he certainly had no intention of getting clean, either. Hearing the commotion as Tori entered the house, he stepped to the door of the living area to watch as she came through the narrow passage and headed to the stairs.

He could tell by the way she walked she had been drinking, but she hid it pretty well. Reaching the bottom, the girl turned the corner too quickly, and leaned her shoulder against the wall to hold herself up.

Laughing to himself as he stroked his lengthy stubble, he moved up beside her and leaned against the newel post facing her, grinning from ear to ear. Seeing him present himself in front of her, Tori scowled. She had not liked the guy from the instant she met him, and having him speak to her at that moment infuriated her. "Get out of my way," she hissed, trying to sound menacing and squinting at him for effect. "I'm going to bed; I have to work tomorrow."

Gazing at his watch, he nodded in an exaggerated fashion, then leaned closer to her, "Its six pm, love. Think you might like some company?"

Confused for a moment, she reached up to steady herself by grasping his forearm. She straightened for the climb, and leaned close enough their faces almost touched; dropping into Spanish she told him to stay away from her.

Taking a few deep breaths, she climbed the run with ease, Enrique standing at the bottom step, enjoying the way her rear end swayed as she moved. He continued to grin to himself as he made his way back into the living room, impressed she had spoken in his native language and thinking, *I'm gonna need to get me some of that.*

Tori made it into her room, closing the door behind her. Leaning back against it, she allowed her body to slide down until she sat on the floor. Grabbing her boot, she pulled hard, trying to get undressed before she was too inebriated to remove her clothing.

A few minutes later, she hauled herself up onto her bed. Having successfully removed her boots, pants, and shirt, she sat in her bra, socks and panties, while panting from the effort it had required. Her head spinning, she knew the blackness would fall any minute.

Managing to get the bra unhooked, she staggered over to her dresser and selected her sleeping shorts and tee. She pulled them on, noticing the scar on her left breast as she worked the shirt into place. Reaching up with her right hand, she massaged the spot through the thin material. Turning to the closet, she maneuvered her way into the corner she had become accustomed to using for sleeping. Relieved to finally be in her favorite spot, she leaned her head against the wall and gasped for air, trying to catch her breath from the struggle.

Calming down, her mind raced back to the last time she had been drunk, and she combed through the events that had occurred only three short months before, inside a farmhouse in Iowa. There she had spent her last night with the Dragons, the last night of their lives. The night she murdered them.

Unexpectedly, a flood of sadness overcame her, sitting alone in the closet. The Dragons had been a terrible blot on society, beaten her, raped her, and forced her to hurt and kill other people. Deep down, she had told herself many times that they had gotten what they deserved. Sitting there, alone in the world, she no longer felt certain she believed it.

The Dragons had also been the only family she had ever known. They had raised her, and been her constant companions as long as she could remember, teaching her everything they knew. A tear fell from her soft blue orb and landed on her bare leg as she tried to stem the flow in vain. *And now they're gone, just as Henry's gone, just as Eli's gone.*

Tori sat in her drunken state, allowing the tears to flow freely as she remembered how she had searched the farmhouse, drinking every drop of liquor she could find, after the Dragons were dead. She had hoped it would be enough, and she would never have to face another day. But it hadn't been enough, or they had been discovered too soon. Either way, she still lived and breathed. The darkness overtook her as she cried, and for a few short hours, she was at peace.

The alarm woke her at 5:00 am, as usual. Stumbling over to shut it off, Tori could feel her head pounding, and she held it with her left hand, trying to stop the spinning. Making it to the bathroom, she managed to shut the door and leaned over the toilet, sent into a spasm of heaving until nothing remained to bring up. She knelt over the toilet for a moment, looking down into the rancid mess before she found the silver handle to wash it away.

She wriggled her way out of her soiled night clothes and slid over into the shower stall, kneeling on the floor. The tile felt good beneath her, and she reached above her head with her right hand and pushed the lever to release the spray. Instantly hit with an ice cold cascade that knocked the wind out of her, she sprang up, onto her knees, trying desperately to adjust the handle so the water would warm a little.

Leaning against the wall beneath the handle and panting deeply, she allowed the water to run down over her nakedness for several minutes before she tried to stand. Eventually, she used the soap to remove the smeared makeup from her face, and gave the rest of her body a haphazard wash, as well.

Reaching over, she cut off the flow and stood dripping for several more minutes. Grasping her towel, she dried her face and body, saving her long thick tresses for last. Her head still swam, and the reality then hit her; she had not brought any clean clothes, and they were all back in her room.

Gingerly picking up her sleepwear between her index finger and thumb, she realized her shower would be a moot point if she put them back on. Dropping them beside the toilet to retrieve later, she wrapped the towel around her body, and prepared to slip back to her sanctuary.

Shutting off the light, she opened the door a crack and listened. The rest of the house silent, she slowly eased her way out, and tried to peer up the stairs that led to the men's floor, knowing Bob would be descending any time for his morning coffee.

Taking a few silent steps, a shape moved in front of her, hands clamping onto her arms and pinning her against the wall that stood between her door and that of the bathroom. Breathing deeply, she tried to remain calm, hearing a very low voice mumbled, "Well, well, well, look what we have heres." The hands released her arms, but he remained standing close enough, she could feel his breath as it brushed her face.

Clutching the towel that covered her bare flesh, Tori leaned the back of her head against the wall to slow the spin and tried to steady her breathing. Enrique slowly came into focus as her eyes adjusted to the darkness, and she could see him grinning at her, his eyes shifting down to take in her tall frame.

Reaching up with his right hand, he laid his palm against her left cheek, tracing the lower edge of her scar with his thumb. She stiffened at the action, realizing it had been exposed with the removal of her makeup.

"Relax, baby girl," he whispered, leaning closer to her.

Baby girl? Oh, shit, I know this guy, her chest heaved.

Seeing the scar, it reminded him that he had already had him some of that, and wouldn't mind another helping. "I'm not going to hurts you." His lips touched hers, and for a moment she considered dropping the towel and knocking him away.

However, putting up a fight would only draw attention to them, and in her still drunken state, she didn't want that. She parted her lips, allowing him to kiss her, and he slipped his left hand up and between the ends of the towel she tried to hold closed in front of her.

She seemed taller than the last time he had fucked her, having been over a year since they had last met. His mind sailed back to the few times his crew had met up with the Dragons, and their paths had crossed. Fondling her breast, she did not resist; *but then again, she never resists.*

Enrique knew she liked what they did to her in the dark, *a dirty girl*, the thought made his pulse grow quicker. He gripped her harder, feeling his flesh swelling in his groin. He wanted to take her into her room for a go right then, and would have if he thought they could get away with it.

However, nearing 6:00 am, it wouldn't be long before the entire house was awake. Easing his death-grip on her breast, he massaged it gently again, lifting his lips from hers so he could whisper to her before letting her go. "You work at that record store, right? Maniac something?"

Tori nodded her agreement, remaining silent. He could feel her breath coming in the form of short excited pants, and he continued to take her in, his hand leaving her ample mound to caress the naked skin of her ribs, her waist, and down the front of her flat belly to the soft swirl of hairs below.

He slid his fingers lightly down to her folds of flesh and stroked the trimmed cover in front for a moment. She relaxed her right leg, allowing him to part her soft folds and his fingers to penetrate the wet hollow hidden beneath. She closed her eyes and exhaled deeply as he fondled her. "What time you gets off tonight, baby girl?"

Thinking for a moment, she considered lying to him, and then quickly realized, *I'm in no position for games.* Stammering slightly, she replied, "We close at eight. I can leave about eight-thirty, after locking everything up." His thumb massaged the small bead beneath the hairs, causing her brain to go fuzzy, and she met his gaze as she relaxed into his caress.

Enrique smiled again, nodding his agreement with that assessment, bringing his moist fingers to his mouth to taste her. In a low voice he confirmed the deal, "That's good, baby, I'll pick you up at eight-thirty then, introduce you to my new crew."

Kissing her deeply again, he pressed the full front of himself against her, so she could feel his hardness through the towel. Then he kissed the tip of her nose, released her, and headed up the stairs, Tori watching him from the wall as he went. As soon as he disappeared, she slid down the passage into her own room, her heart beating like kettle drums in her ears, and closed the door behind her.

Sinking to the floor on her knees, she cursed herself for not recognizing him when he first came into the house. Enrique Dominguez held a position in the Scorpions, a group much like the Dragons. A lower member, his presence there was a mystery.

Unsure what he meant, with his yammering about a new crew, she knew full well he could not have just walked away, any more than she or any other member of the Dragons could have done. What's worse, alone, she did not have the protection of her own group of misfits. *So they have found me, faster than I anticipated they would.*

On her knees, her arms crossing her chest, Tori sat inhaling deeply for several minutes. She rocked back and forth, considering what to do. She could go and tell Brandon and Sharon. Of course, then she would have to explain how she had gotten her hands on the bottle with no ID and broke a house rule by drinking it. Not to mention involving the couple could put them in danger, and the girl didn't want that.

For an instant, she considered calling Chicago, before she recalled the phone call that started the whole mess. The fact that she could not reach Eli or Debra, only left Agent Godfry, who was too by the book and Warren La Buff, who hated her. Running her fingers through her damp waves, Tori realized she had very few options to choose from.

After running through every scenario she could think of, she believed the only way out was to work her way through it. *Meet Enrique after work, do what I have to do to keep everyone safe if I can;* and figure out what to do about her new problem and his crew along the way.

She decided she definitely needed another knife and would like a gun, as well. Dressing quickly, she headed back to the bathroom to re-cover her face and clean up her mess before anyone saw it and became suspicious.

After making herself presentable, she headed downstairs, putting on a smile to add weight to her story. Enrique sat at the short bar that separated the kitchen from the dining, and he eyed her closely as she gathered her water and fruit from the fridge.

Sharon returned the smile, a bit relieved that the young woman looked so chipper. She had mentioned to Brandon before bed she believed the girl might have been drunk. Seeing her now, she considered the possibility she could have been mistaken.

Tori gave the group a quick story about having been down for several days, and the long night of rest seemed to have done the trick. Finally, she announced she needed to run a few errands before work, and would see everyone late that night. With a quick wave, she darted out the door and headed down the drive.

Glancing at the garage again, she wished she had been more diligent on the bike repair, as having it to get away on in a hurry might have come in handy. *Let's just hope I don't have to run,* she consoled herself.

Making her way to the grocery, Tori called for a taxi to pick her up. It only took a few minutes for the yellow cab to find her, and she rapidly climbed in with a fast look around to see if anyone had noticed. Giving the driver the address, she leaned back nervously in the seat.

It had been almost a year since their last visit to LA, but she felt fairly certain she knew where she could get what she needed. Of course, at the moment she would place her order and find out how much it would cost her; the hard part would be coming up with the cash.

Same Old Life

Riding in a taxi, Tori allowed her mind to sift through the events of the last twenty-four hours. Amazing how quickly she had gotten sucked back into her same old life. A stab of sadness touched her heart as she remembered Henry's words, *"You're gonna have a different life, baby girl."*

She told herself she was trying, but deep down, she knew she wasn't trying nearly hard enough. Just before they reached her destination, she made herself a solemn vow; *if I survive this, I'm going to get clean and do what I should have done. I'm going to do it for me, and no one but me.*

Sliding out of the cab, she gave the driver her best smile, "Would you mind waiting for me? I shouldn't be more than a few minutes."

Snatching the cash from her hand, he quipped, "Not in this neighborhood. Good luck!"

Tori sighed as the brake lights shone briefly before he pulled back out onto the street and drove away. *Guess that means getting a cab out of here won't be easy either,* she thought to herself as she entered the run down building.

Holding herself up straight, she braced herself and made her way through the dark hallway, noticing how little had changed since her last visit to the bad part of town. Deep down, she almost felt at home in the dilapidated building, her heart beginning to beat faster as she climbed the stairs. Making her way to the third floor, she moved to the end of the hall, ghosts from the past showing her the way.

Eddie had brought her there once before, when they had come into town and realized they needed some supplies to complete a job. The gang who took refuge in the gutted building consisted of a nasty group of people, but they had connections, and had come through easily when the Dragons had been in a bind. Standing in front of door 317, she tapped lightly, causing it to swing open. Cautiously, she leaned inside, calling out if anyone were home.

In an instant, a shotgun appeared in her face. The young black man holding it trembled from the adrenaline, and he demanded she identify herself.

Tori didn't flinch, responding calmly, "Tori Farrell, Eddie Farrell's girl."

The young man pulled his weapon, "You here alone?"

Without batting an eyelash, she replied, "Yep. We have a problem, and I need your help."

He led her into the apartment, where she discovered the man she had come to see lying on an old couch, holding a blood soaked compress to his belly. "We got problems round heya, too," he stated as if he were talking about the weather.

As she took in the scene, Tori's jaw fell in disbelief. Without hesitation, she let her jacket plummet to the floor and pushed up her white sleeves. Dropping to her knees beside him, she lifted the towel enough to see blood oozing from a long gash in his side.

"You've lost a lot of blood," she whispered softly.

"Tell me sumfin I do'n know," he replied, followed by a short, spastic laugh and a moan from the pain it produced.

Tori frowned, reaching up to lay her hand against his cheek and neck to assess his vitals. "You have medical supplies?" she asked anxiously, her eyes wide with concern.

Turning slightly, he gave the boy a nod, and upon standing, she followed him to the bathroom in the back where the emergency kit hid beneath the sink. Rummaging quickly, she located fresh gauze, medical tape and a suture kit. She also grabbed a couple of bottles of rubbing alcohol, and asked the boy, "You have any clean water, like distilled or bottled?"

Nodding, he ran to fetch them while she made her way back to the older man on the couch. Laying the equipment on the floor next to him, she tried to sound calm as she explained, "You know, last time we were here I never caught your name."

He smiled a toothy grin and spouted, "Dats cause I neva dropped it. I'm D'Shawn. Dats my boy, Lamont," he indicated the young man who had returned with five bottles of drinking water.

"Well, nice to meet the both of you," her smile barely touched her tense lips. "Lamont, do you have any clean sheets or towels?"

Again, the boy dashed away to get what she required. Carefully removing the compress, Tori began to inspect his wound, finding it to be long, but not very deep. The relief showed on her face, as she realized if she stitched him up, he would probably be ok.

Lamont returned with a stack of towels, so she grabbed one to lay along the edge of the couch to catch the liquid as she irrigated the area with the water, and then finished by cleaning the wound with the alcohol. "By the way, this's gonna hurt," she warned softly.

D'Shawn nodded his understanding, panting through gritted teeth while she worked. As soon as she had it washed, she folded the flesh together, and laid another clean towel along the gash, instructing Lamont to hold pressure against it for a minute.

Opening the suture kit, Tori pulled out the forceps and needle, and began to piece the flesh back together. She had put stitches in members of her crew many times over the years, so her hands were steady as she worked her way across the opening. Reaching the end, she tied off the nylon and clipped the line with the scissors.

"How yo' know how to do dat?" D'Shawn asked her directly.

Still kneeling, she leaned back on her heels, drawing in a deep breath, "I've had lots of practice," her smile genuine.

He nodded again as she used the gauze and tape to cover the wound, and began to explain what he would need to do to care for it over the next few days. Finishing up, she stood, looking down at her bloodied white tee and considered what to do about it, as she could not go into work like that. D'Shawn, feeling better already, began his cross examination.

"Now, why yo' heya girl? And where's yo' man? Last time I seen the two o' you, he waddn't abo' to leave yo' alo'."

Tori chuckled at his description of Eddie and his attachment to her. Doing her best to explain, she decided the truth, as far as she could go with it, would be her best option.

"Well, Eddie, my man, is dead. We ran into some trouble, and I came to see if you could help me get some weapons and tools." She paused to see what his reaction would be, and his eyes widened a bit as he considered her words carefully.

D'Shawn knew she must be in one hell of a mess if she'd come to him for help. Sticking his lips out for a moment, he allowed her to stew before he asked, "Wut kinda weapons?"

She gave him her short list. "I'm hoping to get a knife, preferably an OTF, but if not, any switchblade will do. I also need a pocket nine, with an extra clip if I can get it, and a box of bullets, any brand or type that will work in the pistol." He nodded as she spoke, so she pushed for the item that would be a longshot, "And lastly, I'd like a set of lock pick tools; five or nine pieces at the largest."

Lamont stood with hands behind his back, looking down

at his father, who studied the girl in silence. "You wanna holsta' fo' tha nine?" he asked her after a few moments.

"No, no," she shook her head briskly, "Just the pistol would be great."

D'Shawn looked over his shoulder at his son, and with a wave of his hand, the boy darted off again. Only gone about fifteen minutes, it seemed like an eternity to Tori as she looked around the rundown apartment and surveyed the clutter it contained.

When the boy returned, he did, in fact, have everything she had required, plus a new shirt for her to boot. Tori stared down at the items in amazement, "What do I owe you?"

"Nuthin'," D'Shawn replied weakly, indicating his freshly patched wound with an open palm, as if thanking her for fixing him up, "Lamont'll make shore you git back down t' yur taxi saftely."

She smiled sheepishly as she gathered the items, "I'm afraid that my taxi left me."

D'Shawn only gave a wave of his hand, smiling as he sent her on her way; Lamont disappeared a final time, returning a few moments later to wait patiently for his charge.

Preparing to leave, Tori pulled her jacket on and gave the knife a quick flick test. She grinned widely as the blade popped out the end. Hitting the release again, the steel shaft snapped back into its sheath, and she shoved it into her boot, pulling her pant leg down to cover it.

Pushing the Beretta Nano into her right hand pocket, she put the tools, clip and bullets into her left. Leaning over, she kissed her benefactor on the forehead while caressing his cheek one last time. "Take care of yourself, D'Shawn," she breathed. She then followed Lamont back down through the darkness and out into the front of the building.

She then realized her presence had not gone unnoticed, as

several people were watching as she exited the building, but to her relief a yellow cab, in fact, waited for her. Lamont closed the door with a thud, and the driver pulled away, asking for the address. She gave him the name of the supermarket close to the house, and then sank back into the seat to enjoy the ride.

Peering down at the shirt she still held in her hands, she checked the size and decided it would fit. Sliding out of her jacket, she pulled her blood covered original over her head, and noted the driver adjusted the mirror to get a better view, which made her smile.

The man swallowed hard when he noticed the large bite mark on her left breast, but made no comment. Tori tugged the new shirt over her head, reaching beneath her dark waves to free her hair from being trapped inside. Although short sleeved, no one would notice if she kept her jacket on, and it would have to do.

Sitting back and watching the scenery as it passed, Tori felt thankful she had made it in and out of unfriendly territory unscathed. Her jacket lying across her lap, she could feel the outline of her new toy in the pocket and the familiar pressure of her knife inside her boot.

In retrospect, it didn't feel so bad having her old life back. Remembering the vow she made to herself, she knew someday she would do exactly that, but at the moment, she intended to enjoy herself while she was there.

One Man's Fantasy

Exiting her yellow chariot at the supermarket, Tori stopped next to the garbage barrel out front, and shoved her bloodied garment under a few layers of refuse. She then scurried inside to purchase a few supplies and get back to the house as quickly as she could. She would have to hurry to avoid being late for work. Thinking quickly, she grabbed a roll of duct tape, a box of tampons and an extra-large box of feminine napkins, paying for all at the counter.

Walking back towards the house, she tore open the larger box first, throwing some of the pads out onto the ground. Taking the gun from her pocket, she slipped it down into the box and covered the top with the remainder of the pads, making it appear she had opened the box to remove one. Next, she opened the box of tampons, hiding the clip and bullets inside them the same way.

She shoved the small roll of tape into her pocket, feeling confident she would pass inspection if anyone chose to search her. Inside the kitchen, the small gathering generally looked surprised to see her. She made quite a show of her purchases as Enrique sat watching her, but she knew full well being on her period wouldn't deter him if he really wanted to fuck her.

Running up the stairs, she took a quick shower, and stuck one of the pads to her panties, hating the way it made a lumpy feel between her legs. Later, if she had to remove her pants she could always claim she must have only been spotting to explain its pristine condition. Going back to her room, she closed the door and dumped the contents of the box onto her bed.

Lifting the nightstand, she slid the clock and lamp onto the bed, and flipped it upside down. Using the duct tape, she attached the pistol, box of bullets, and extra clip to the bottom, which stood only about three inches off the floor; that meant someone would either have to get down on all fours or flip it over to see it.

Replacing the small piece of furniture to its location, she shifted the clock and lamp back into place, and returned her feminine products to their boxes. Finally, slipping the lock pick kit into her inner jacket pocket next to her sunglasses, she felt ready to head to work. Bounding back down the stairs, she cursed under her breath as she realized she didn't have enough time to get there on schedule. Only giving Enrique a cursory glance, she suspected he watched her as she left.

To her surprise, Brandon waited for her in the driveway with the car, "Hey; hop in." Climbing into the front seat, a shocked expression on her face, he smiled and continued teasingly, "Even you deserve a break once in a while." She smiled her thanks at the older man, and he dropped her off at the single door with one minute to spare.

Terry looked up as she entered, his reading glasses sitting down on the end of his nose while he worked. Pulling them off, he grinned, "Wow, I was beginning to worry. It isn't like you to be just on time."

Tori giggled back, swinging her hair while she made her way around the glass counter. "Sorry," she murmured, "I had female problems and had to run home for a shower and change before I came in."

He laughed at her honesty, thinking most girls would have made up a lie before admitting that was the reason they were late.

She made a trip around the store to see how things looked, and found Max and Keith in the back leaning on a wall. "Don't you two have something to do around here?" she demanded crossly.

Max rolled his eyes, and Keith gave her a dirty look, but both exited through the double doors to the floor. Unlocking the office, Tori pulled her jacket off and laid it over the chair; then opening the safe, she pulled out the deposit for Terry to take to the bank. Locking everything, she herself returned to the front.

Laying the bag on the counter next to him, she suddenly felt a wave of attachment wash over her, and she realized that somehow, Terry had become her friend. Dropping into Russian, she inquired playfully, "What're you working on?"

He replied softly, "Just looking at some parts for a new guitar I may be building for Brian Madson. He called me this morning with some specs, and I want to get the parts in case he decides to give me the go ahead on it."

Tori knew Brian Madson played the guitar in a band called *Indelible*. They had been pretty successful for about five years, and were going to be in the shop later in the year for a big promotion that they were putting on for their new album.

She nodded her approval, then nudged his elbow, pointing at the bag. Glancing over at it, he sighed his agreement that it needed to be done, and the ordering would have to wait. Taking it, he tossed her a wave, "I'll be back later," and headed out.

As soon as he left, the two boys came over to the counter to razz her a bit. Their latest theory as to why Terry gave her all the easy jobs fresh in their minds, they could not wait to run it by her. She gave the pair an icy stare, causing Keith to laugh before he proclaimed that Tori must be spending her nights over at Terry's place, instead of the halfway house.

Her jaw dropped when she heard this, not realizing they even knew where she lived. "And how exactly did you come by that information?" she demanded.

The pair fell into fits of laughter, and Keith taunted her, "It's impossible to have secrets from someone who really wants to know."

She shook her head at the boys, *morons,* and let it go, shooing them back to work. The rest of the day went smoothly, and Terry did return for a short while to finish ordering the parts. Then, with a friendly nod, he bade her good night, leaving her alone with the young men and the customers for the rest of the evening.

Tori felt fine until around 7:00 pm. Grasping they would be closing soon, she began to feel her chest tighten and her heart rate climb in anticipation or dread; at this point she couldn't tell which. Running her fingers through her hair nervously, she made sure the guys were straightening up and getting ready to close.

A few minutes before 8:00 pm, she shut down the instrument register, and then locked the doors to close out the other. By a quarter after, everything had been completed, and they were ready leave.

Letting Keith and Max out and locking the door behind them, Tori looked up and down the street; the lump in her stomach rapidly ballooned with her date nowhere in sight. She decided to move around to the double doors, and then made her way back in an anxious pacing motion.

On the third trip, she met Enrique outside the single door. He walked right up to her and casually looped his arm around her waist. Sliding back hastily, she explained that some of her coworkers may be spying on her, and they needed to be careful until they were somewhere more private.

In silent agreement, he spun around haphazardly on one foot, looking for anyone that might be looking at him. Not seeing anyone, he indicated for her to follow with a curled finger and a sly smile, and they crossed the street, stepping up to his motorcycle.

Sliding onto it behind him, Tori shivered as she could feel the familiar hum that made her female parts tingle. Grabbing her long hair, she twisted it and pulled it down inside her jacket to protect it from whipping around as they rode.

It turned out, they didn't have far to go, and he pulled in beside a little bar, very much like the ones the Dragons had frequented so much of their time on the road. Once inside, Enrique twirled around, grabbing her around her hips with both arms and lifting her feet to swing her in a playful circle.

The behavior surprised her a little, and she clung to his shoulders to hang on. Resting her feet back on the ground, she became aware that she smiled at him uncontrollably, and he kissed her gently on the lips. He rested his forehead against hers in an intimate fashion, exhaling deeply.

Tori felt confused, not really sure what to make of his behavior. Her arms still draped around his neck, she raised her hand to caress the back of his head and run her fingers through his short dark hair. The movement excited her, and for a moment she felt her brain go fuzzy, his chocolate brown eyes seeming to pull her in.

"You know; I've been thinking about you all day," he spoke in a low voice, "And I just wants you alls to myself."

Tori's heart began to thump in her chest as they continued to sway to the beat of the jukebox. She made no reply, and simply studied his handsome features and coy grin. *He's quite the charmer*, she mused; not something she had ever run into in her past life, unless Eli counted.

"You don't know it, but you're my fantasy, baby girl.

I've dreamed about you a long times now." He smiled at her, and was exactly right; she didn't know it… and even as he said it, she really didn't believe it.

Hold on Tight

Tori might not have believed what he said, but she had been around enough to know better than to say so. Instead, she played along, laying a long deep kiss on him that made her own knees weak.

Slowly working her further into the room, he opened up, "Ok, you gotta tells me how the hells you got away from the Dragons. Last time I seen you, things was pretty tense between our two groups, and I hate to says it, but you was right in the middle o' the hassle."

"How do you mean?" she asked in authentic surprise.

Looking down at her luscious lips, he ran his hands up and down her back, trying to decide exactly how to put it. Finally, he spit it out. "You remember Brett Spears?" he asked quietly.

Tori nodded, recognizing the head of the Scorpions.

"Brett put an offer on the table to buy you from Eddie. I mean a hells of an offer... 300K."

Tori stopped moving in stunned silence, her surprise evidenced by her gaping mouth.

Thinking he might have offended her, Enrique grasped a few stray hairs and smoothed them down. Gently, he continued running his fingers through her ebony locks to soothe her, and whispered, "I'm sorry, I thought you knew." He had dropped into Spanish and obviously wanted to appease her.

Clamping her mouth shut, Tori drew a deep breath and

released it slowly, laying her head against his shoulder and falling back into their sway. At only a couple of inches taller than herself, she couldn't help thinking he fit her size perfectly.

No, she hadn't known. But the discovery put many other things into perspective. Henry had told her he intended to get another group to kill the Dragons; clearly, that group the Scorpions. Of course, if Brett had wanted to own her, it would have complicated her escape to whoever he had alluded to that night in the café, the one who would be looking after her.

The couple continued to turn, occasionally sharing a kiss, while their hands moved easily over one another's bodies in a familiar manner. If anyone had been watching them, they would have thought the two were lovers by the way they held one another, and Tori soon became lost in the comfort his actions produced.

Growing relaxed, she admitted to being alone and that the Dragons were gone. She explained that she would have died herself if she had not been found in time and rushed to the hospital. When he asked what happened to them, she claimed not to know; she only knew that she had been drunk, and when she awoke in the hospital, the Dragons were all dead. If he didn't believe her, he gave no indication as she spoke, and she smiled inwardly that her version of the past had been approved.

She then told him about what had happened in Chicago, but left out the part where she had betrayed The Organization, as that would have been a problem, as well. Finally, she explained that the Feds stuck her in the halfway house for six months, hinting at punishment for being uncooperative, but they had promised after that she would be released.

He listened intently, continuing to run his hands over her

body as she spoke. His touch made her dizzy, and she allowed herself to briefly imagine the two of them alone, and naked, in a more private location.

"Looks like we're both home free then," he commented offhandedly at her news.

In the back of her mind, Tori doubted his really being free. However, she wanted to believe her new friend, needing someone she could trust; he didn't offer any details, and she didn't pry, finding herself lost in the sweetness of his words and the tenderness with which he held her.

The time passed too quickly, and at 11:00 pm, she reluctantly pointed out they had to be back at the house by midnight, and it would be better if they did not return together. Enrique had to agree, and so they mounted up and headed towards home. As they rode, Tori leaned forward, her arms tight around his chest. It occurred to her that her ruse might have worked, and her period trick kept him at bay.

He stopped the bike two blocks from the house so she could walk and make it in plenty of time before he arrived just before midnight. He remained sitting on his bike while she slid off and turned to lean in beside him, kissing him goodnight. She decided to test her theory and whispered, "I'm sorry about getting my period."

He emitted a small laugh, hugging her playfully while running his hand down the crack of her rear end, "That's ok, baby. We'll have plenty of time when it's over." He grinned at her, arms holding her firmly as he spoke, "We're free now, remember? You and me."

Tori's heart made a strange leap at his words. Reluctant to walk away, her hair bounced as she trotted the rest of the way home.

Enrique waited until she had disappeared into the dark, then reached inside his inner pocket and pulled out a small flip phone. Opening it, he pressed the send key and dialed the only number he ever called. A male voice picked up on the other end, and Enrique gave the voice a quick update, "Yeah, I got her... Yeah, she'll be good to go, I promise. I'll check in again later." He ended the call by flicking the phone shut. Starting the engine, he rolled smoothly up to the front of the house, and dismounted to head inside.

Tori had entered the dwelling minutes before, finding Sharon and Brandon waiting for her at the dining room table. Realizing she still wore a broad smile, she quickly wiped it away at the sight of the couple. On the table in front of them sat a small, hand held Breathalyzer machine. Looking down guiltily, she felt extremely grateful the pair only spent the night dancing. "Well," she scratched her chin tensely; "I guess you guys don't trust me after all."

"It's not about trust," Sharon stood slowly; "It's about being sure."

She held out the small machine, and Tori placed the clear plastic tube in her mouth and blew. A few seconds later, the LED screen lit up 0.0, and she could see the look of relief on both of their faces. She smiled awkwardly, and asked if she could be excused. The couple laughed anxiously, as they sent her on up to her room.

Sharon sat back down, and Tori realized they were waiting for Enrique. She knew he had not had a drink in the time she had been with him, and she only hoped he had abstained before that, as well.

Climbing the stairs, she began to replay the nights events in her mind, surprised what a difference a couple of hours could make. She undressed and slipped into her night shorts and tee. Hearing footsteps in the hall, she opened her door to go to the bathroom as Enrique appeared on the stairs and turned onto the next level.

He could see the relief on her face as she gazed up at him, and he quietly gave her a thumbs-up signal and a smile as he trudged along.

Going on into her bathroom, Tori could feel her face flushed with excitement. Her smile quickly disappeared when she saw the spot of blood on the should-have-been pristine pad she placed there before work. *Damn it.* Her periods never had been right since the incident in Scottsville, Texas, when Eddie had given her an abortion with a clothes hanger five years before.

Feeling a little deflated, Tori made her way back to her bedroom, and sank into the corner of her closet to sleep. Thinking about how Enrique had acted that morning, she recalled how his actions had frightened her. Terrified her, in fact, to the point she had gone to one of the worst places she had ever been in her life, and she had been in some pretty bad places, just to arm herself.

In retrospect, she felt pretty foolish due to the loving way he had held her. Drifting off to sleep, she could still feel the warmth of his embrace and longed to be lying beside him, curled in his arms, rather than crouching in the dark corner like a coward. *Oh well, at least now I have the equipment, and at some point it may still come in handy.*

Jumping up when the alarm went off, Tori threw on her running clothes and shoes quite hurriedly, and as she exited her chamber, had a peek up the stairs and about the landing to see if Enrique might be hanging about. Not seeing anything, she went on with her routine, trotting quietly down and out the back door.

Running to the playground, Tori made it through twelve rounds of twelve with ease, and then turned back to the house in a full sprint. She could not wait to get back, hoping to catch a glimpse of Enrique before she left for work. But, as she climbed the veranda steps, the thought occurred to her they would have to be discreet, even if she did get to see him.

Opening the door, she could see Bob sitting at the table,

drinking his coffee as usual. Next to him sat her new obsession. Her heart rate doubled as she closed the door and heard his sultry voice bid her good morning.

"Good morning," she answered nice and loud, and with a quick wave she headed on up the stairs to shower and dress for the day. Putting on another of the thick pads, in case she wasn't finished, she opened the door to find Enrique leaning against the wall where he had held her trapped the morning before.

Stepping back inside the bathroom, he darted in after her and shut the door behind himself. Instantly, they were caught up in an embrace, his hands running eagerly over her body. Tori found herself responding in kind, hoping she would be able to perform when the night came. After a few minutes of groping, he broke off their kiss to get down to business.

"What time you gets off?" he whispered eagerly.

"Uhh, four pm today. I'll meet you at the bar as quick as I can." Her eyes sparkled when her fingers caressed his hair line, and she tightened her grip on him as she enjoyed the rush.

He smiled, kissing her nose, "Have a good day, baby."

Reluctantly releasing him, Tori exited the bathroom first to have a look around, and then motioned to him the coast was clear. He went up to the next level, while she went down to have breakfast. Leaving as soon as she finished her fruit, she walked along drinking her water and swaying her hair merrily. She could not ever remember feeling the joy that consumed her, not at any time in her life.

A few hours later, Terry had an odd feeling about the girl as soon as he entered the store. He could see Tori talking to a couple of guys, showing them guitars over at the instrument counter, and grinning from ear to ear. He had never seen her act the way she was that day, and he stood for a while watching her as she sold each of them a custom job. The two men left the store, equally as happy, and Terry felt warm inside, thinking that his efforts to improve her self-esteem might be paying off.

Going to the back, he collected the deposit, and then gave her a wave as he headed to the bank. Returning a short time later, he decided to have a little talk with her about her responsibilities. Telling Max to keep an eye on the front, he led her to the back, where they could speak in private.

"I've been thinking," he started out in a low voice, "That you might be ready to learn a bit more about running the store." He waited for her reaction. She smiled, eagerly nodding her agreement, and they spent the rest of the afternoon going over invoices as he introduced her to the accounts payable, or AP, side of the bookkeeping.

By 4:00 pm, Tori felt a wreck, ready to go and meet up with Enrique, the word *boyfriend* tickling the back of her mind. She had never had one, and the thought burned and excited her the closer the end of her shift came. Fondly, she recalled the previous night, *"You and me," he said. I've never been part of a 'we' before,* and she liked the way it felt.

Noticing the time, Terry closed up the notebook he kept the invoices in and told her jokingly, "Get out of here and don't come back until tomorrow."

Tori agreed she would not be back until 8:00 am to open the store, and headed out the double glass doors in great haste. Speed walking the few blocks to the tiny building, and stepping inside out of the afternoon sun, Tori anxiously folded her shades and slid them into her interior pocket to have a look around. Spotting Enrique, he sat at a table in the back watching her, and she rushed over to throw her arms around him.

She had pounced on his lap, gripping him eagerly, and he slid his hand down, rubbing the crack of her rear end playfully. His hand lingered, and he could tell something had changed with the way she felt.

Smiling deviously, she nodded and whispered, "Yup, all better," leaning forward to nuzzle his neck.

Immediately, Enrique flagged down the barkeep, asking if they could use his office for a bit. The older man waved them on, and Tori grasped Enrique's hand as he led her towards the rear of the small bar and into the office that stood in the back corner. The room seemed cramped for their first time, but it would have to do she guessed; at least they would get to be together.

Stepping inside the small space, Enrique dropped his lips next to her ear and whispered, "You better holds on tight, baby girl. I'm gonna steal your heart tonight."

Tori laughed at how corny the line sounded, thinking to herself, *it's too late, baby - you already have.*

Love Thy Neighbor

Tori could feel her heart thumping with excitement as they surveyed the small room. The office, in reality a cubicle barely large enough to house the single desk, chair, and bookcase that overfilled the tiny space, would be cramped for maneuvering. Switching on the small lamp that sat on the desk, she reached over and shut off the harsh overhead light. Turning her attention to her new lover, she allowed him to undress her, and returned his warm kisses eagerly.

Sliding his hands over her soft skin, he lifted her shirt over her head, and then unlatched her bra with a single practiced movement, pulling it forward and allowing it to drop to the floor. She stood bathed in the soft glow of the tiny bulb, and he ran his right hand up her side, and then cupped her left breast so he could run his thumb across her scar.

Bending over, he took the nipple into his mouth, sucking on it, and then nipping at it gently. Tori arched her back, pushing her chest out for easier access, causing her hair to hang down in a dark cascade of silk. He reached up grasping a small handful and tugging it playfully before releasing it as she looked at him hungrily.

Pulling at the front of her jeans, he unbuttoned and unzipped them in a quick motion, and a gasp of pleasure escaped her. He slid his hands over her round rear end as he pushed them down, cupping her and pulling her hard against his swelling mound of flesh. Tori panted, as he continued to run his hands across her nakedness, freeing her legs and feet from her pants and boots.

He had been with her before, but she had no recollection of the event, making him all new to her. Eager to please him, she wanted to remove his clothing, as he had stripped hers away. Beginning with his shirt, she lifted the garment up, and he raised his arms for her before she let it fall on top of hers.

Tori noticed the pile of material covering the floor like a mat beneath their feet. Grasping the front of his pants, her excited fingers couldn't get the button to slide out of the hole, so he grabbed it with one hand and released it for her. Reaching, she worked his pants down a short way, and then plunged her hands inside, searching for his hardened treasure.

Clutching him with her left hand, she could feel the fullness of him, and appreciated the size of him. Holding onto the waist of his pants on either side, she pulled down with both hands, and he sprang up in front of her face, hard as a rock.

She slid her fingers around him firmly, and stroked him back and forth as she licked the salty ooze that had begun to leak from him. Running his hand through her hair, he rubbed the back of her head, encouraging her to take him, and she easily slid his full length into her mouth and down her throat, working him for several minutes while he groaned loudly.

When his grasp on her head tightened, Tori removed him from her mouth, holding his shaft with her hand and squeezing him for a moment. She could feel him pulse within her grip. Looking up at him from her knees, there glinted a wild look in his eyes, and her warm female folds began to ache, moist with desire for him.

Pushing him back, she stood, and he dropped onto the plain wooden chair behind him. Moving to straddle him, she took him inside of her wet chasm, and he grabbed her round butt cheeks, lifting her up and down as she slid on top of him. They worked that way for several minutes, the pounding motion becoming heavier as she moved above him.

Working her body by lifting herself with her legs, she felt her insides growing tighter, anticipating her imminent release. While their bodies collided, she became aware that he fingered her other opening as she moved, pushing his digits deeper and harder inside of her. Reaching back, she could feel that he had two or three fingers inside of her.

Realizing her awareness of his intentions excited him immeasurably. Sitting down on him firmly and holding still, she tried to force him to remove the offending digits, which he resisted momentarily with a devilish grin. Sliding them out, he grabbed her by her cheeks and lifted her completely off of himself, sliding her back down with a quick motion that positioned him squarely into the new orifice.

Taken by surprise, Tori sat still on top of him, gasping for breath from his action.

He slid his hands over her body, comforting her and encouraging her to relax. Nuzzling her face with his nose, he whispered, "Just breathe, baby... you know you want this," and his hand slid up her tender ribs and caressed her breast.

She did want to please him, and gave it her best to comply. She could feel her weight slowly forcing him deeper inside, stretching her further, the tinge of discomfort confusing her thoughts and emotions.

Finally, after what seemed like several minutes, her breath returned, and he pulled her against him firmly, squeezing her tightly in his arms. He lifted her and allowed her to drop, slowly fucking her, his breathing coming in deep gasps as he suddenly plunged over the edge.

His release stung her raw skin, and she sat on him while he deflated, allowing him to pet her and whisper to her in his low sticky voice. When she finally stood, she left streaks of blood on him, and his jaw tightened at the sight of it.

Tori could tell he had not meant to hurt her, and she whispered to him, "See? That's what the gel's for." It wasn't a move she would have chosen, but she wasn't about to tell him so; her body belonged to him, and she would never deny him. Instead, she kissed him, sealing the pact between them before letting him go.

Using his underwear, he cleaned himself and tossed them into the trash bin next to the desk. When he stood, their still naked flesh brushing against each other, he pulled her to him and squeezed her tight. His lips breathing against her ear, he whispered tenderly, "My God, baby, I love you."

She could feel him stroking the length of her spine, her nipples tickled by the hair on his chest as she let the words soak into her frazzled being. Looking into his deep brown orbs, she whispered in return, "Really?"

Her eyes brimmed with tears, and he nodded with a smile, "Yeah, I told you, you're my fantasy! I'm crazy about you." He kissed her and caressed her cheek, laughing softly at her surprise. He felt pleased at how easy she had been to convince, like so many girls before her.

The pair took their time getting dressed, enjoying one another's bodies for as long as they could. When both were finally decent, they exited the tiny room to be greeted by cheers from those who had known they had gone in, several jokingly tapping their watches and pointing out their marathon session.

Seeing the lateness of the hour, Tori realized they had indeed taken a long time. However, she felt thoroughly pleased with the outcome, her heart basking in the bliss of his words.

The pair moved to stand at the bar, and she could smell the liquor being dispensed. The odor reminded her of the first time she had tasted it, when shots were poured and placed in front of her, and she had been ordered to drink. She could feel her mouth wet with saliva, and she briefly battled with the urge to knock back a few. Feeling the sting inside of her where Enrique had been, she decided it worth the risk of getting caught, knowing it would dull the ache.

Ordering a triple shot of vodka, she gave him a wink, and then downed it with ease. He stared at her in surprise, but she waved his question away with her hand, "That's enough; I only wanted a taste."

Moving into his arms, the couple spent the remaining two hours holding one another and swaying to the familiar tunes. Of course, she downed a few more triples before they left, and felt pretty good on the ride home, massaging his chest as they rode.

Fortunately, no one was in the kitchen when they slipped inside, one at a time, and she made it to her room unnoticed. Stripping her boots and clothing, Tori sang one of the evening's songs softly to herself. Her mind drifted over the night's events, their nasty sex and the slow dancing that followed.

A loud sigh escaped her as she finally made it into her corner, and she sat running her fingers lightly over her flesh, it still tingling from their activities. Drifting off to sleep, her thoughts still revolved around her latest drug, and she realized she had become completely lost in him.

Up at 5:00 am as usual, Tori was slow on her run and only completed a few sets before heading back to the house. Her mind full, her body ached as she thought about the highlights of the evening before, longing to do them again.

No one had ever said that they loved her, not even Henry, and the words had done something incredible to her. Even though physically exhausted, and her head clouded, her smile could not be wiped away as she fumbled through her routine.

Tori struggled to make it through the day in her

distracted state. She had not had so much as a glimpse of Enrique, which drove her mad. Nothing penetrated her fog, and she was oblivious that her condition would be evident to those around her.

Terry wanted to teach her more about the books, but with her mind elsewhere, she kept making mistakes. He knew it wasn't like her, and he pondered the cause. Choosing to say nothing, he ended the lesson early, "We can do this some other time." Watching her fumble around for another half hour, he finally sent her on her way, laughing at the change in her behavior, and hoping it was only temporary.

Headed for their usual spot, Tori hit the door of the pub eagerly. Once inside, she made her way past the pool table to the stools along the bar in the back, expecting to find him waiting for her. Unable to locate him in the hazy air, she felt a stab of disappointment in her chest before she remembered she had arrived early. Sitting and waiting semi-patiently, she decided to have a drink or two to loosen up a bit for their evening. She could feel the tingle in her lower lip by the time he arrived, and he made it all the way up to her before she noticed him.

Stepping up behind, he slipped his arm around her waist and cooed, "Hello, neighbor." She stared at him blankly, and he smiled, "You know, downstairs neighbor. Loves thy neighbor. Gets it?"

She smiled back, shaking her head at his silliness, then stood to put her arms around him, and they rocked to the music for a while, holding one another close. Soon, their hands became restless, and they were eagerly taking each other in.

Eventually, he motioned to the barkeep and pointed at the office. Getting a thumbs-up, he pushed her towards it, his jeans already tight from their heavy petting. Once they had the door shut, they put on the lamp for light and positioned the chair in the small space.

Drunk, and much more eager to get to the good part, they each peeled their clothes off as if it were a race. With a tipsy giggle, she proclaimed she had won, but only by a pant leg.

Pulling her naked body fully against his, he took the time to caress her warm skin. She ran her fingers up and down his smooth back and across the curly hairs of his chest in anticipation. Noticing his small tube of gel on the desk, she eyed it for a moment, still unsure how she really felt about the way he would use it and her body. Catching her gaze, he picked it up to spin off the cap, and then returned it to the edge of the desk for easy dispensing.

Assuming they were ready to begin, he plunked himself onto the chair, which faced the desk, pulling her down on top of himself. He slid easily into her warm wetness, indeed ready and eager to have him inside her.

Tori moaned loudly with need. She used her legs to push herself up and down on top of him, moving slow, then fast, then slow again, his hard throbbing making her want to scream. Grasping the back of the chair that extended above his shoulders, she used it for leverage and pushed her body forcefully against his, the tip of him hitting a spot that gave her chills.

Pressing on the tube, the gel squirted onto his fingers, and he slid them into her as she worked, then positioned his hand so she essentially caused them to move in and out of her while she worked him on the front side. Tori could feel the way they spread her, preparing her for him, and she relaxed into her desire to please him.

Pulling herself up extra high, she made the switch with a fluid motion, her yearning to satisfy him stronger than any trepidation that she felt. Lowering herself slowly, she could feel him sliding into the new position; dropping her jaw, she wanted to breathe and maintain her focus.

Their eyes locked, his arms squeezed her tightly as she allowed her weight to bring her body down upon him. Catching her breath, she halted in suspended motion, and again he stroked and nuzzled her, whispering to her sweetly as she took him. She slowly inhaled, able to flex her legs enough to move in short, smooth strokes.

Swiftly, he looped his arms up behind her, grasping her shoulders and forcing her down hard upon him. She could feel small shoots of pain at taking all of him in an awkward position, and moaned slightly at the discomfort, while she puffed air lightly and willed herself to accept it.

His whispery voice pleaded with her not to move, "My God, baby, please be still," and he pressed his forehead against her jaw as they focused.

He held her there for several seconds, trying to avoid finishing so soon. Finally, able to allow her to reposition, he lifted her off of him, and grinned, pleased to see this time he came out clean. Rising next to her, he instructed her to kneel on the pile of clothes that lay at their feet, and he pushed her body across the seat of the chair.

Obeying him, the wood felt warm against her belly where he had been sitting, and she smiled at the thought of him, captive to the passions he brought to life within her.

From behind, he applied more of the gel before taking her again, able to make full thrusts as he drove himself against her for several minutes. He noticed she made loud grunts and moans as he moved, slapping against her wetness noisily as he worked. *God she loves the way I fuck her,* he thought to himself, his heart pounding with exhilaration.

Pushed up onto his toes while stooping over, he lay against her, blowing warm air across her ear and whispering to her until he couldn't hold off any longer. Gripping her flesh tightly, his full body jerked in spasms of ecstasy. Holding himself there, he wanted to enjoy being inside her as long as he could, his mouth and hands tasting and touching at will.

His desire spent, he relaxed over her, with their bodies pressed together in the dim light. He could feel her breathing begin to slow, and he nuzzled her back and caressed her sweaty skin. Wisps of long dark hair moved as he exhaled, and he caught them to smooth them into the rest of her silky mane.

The action brought a smile to his lips, and he felt overcome with deep affection for the woman who lay beneath him, panting his name. *You and me, baby. You and me,* he promised her silently, a satiated grin curling his lips.

Lost in the moment, he felt his devotion to her, and he realized he really wanted to keep her for himself. The thought brought a flood of panic into his muddled brain. Sliding himself out, he stood up quickly, leaning back against the wall.

Staring down at her naked curves, his smile disappeared. His heart pounded loudly inside his ears. *No fucking way!* He knew this couldn't be real. *This wasn't supposed to happen.* His mind worked in circles. *You're not allowed to love her!* But he did. Running his fingers through his dark waves, his mind continued to race. *Ho...ly... shit!* He knew he was in trouble.

Feeling him withdraw, Tori tried to bring herself back to reality. Lifting her head, she pushed herself up from the chair she had been draped over, remaining on her knees for a moment to recuperate. Then she stood, facing him with a warm smile.

His brows were furrowed, eyes dark, and he stroked her arms with his palms, looking her up and down. Sensing something wasn't right, her smile faded, "What's wrong?" *Is it my turn? Is he waiting for me?* Her heart thumped loudly, her body petrified at the idea of saying the words she had never spoken.

Licking his lips uncertainly, he stammered for a moment, then pulled her to him and wrapped her in a strong embrace, rocking her side to side. *Jesus Christ, when did this happen? I'm not any different;* at least he hadn't thought he was any different. He had wanted her ever since he laid eyes on her; wanted to own her, as any man in their world would own such a girl.

But the last few weeks had been chaos for Enrique, and he found himself standing in a tiny room, discovering he held something worth more to him than even his own life. *Brett isn't gonna let you keep her, man,* he warned himself. *Why the fuck did you tell him you had her?* The battle raged inside him. Stroking her hair, he choked back a sob as he considered what he had to do.

Tori held him tightly, her hands sliding firmly across his skin in a sweet caress, while she mustered her courage. She felt so tempted to say the words to him. *Is it too soon? I've never said them to anyone,* she blinked rapidly, deathly afraid of what they would mean when she did. *Oh, my God, I'm so scared,* she clung to him, breathing deeply while her thoughts ran wild. *Come on, you can do this,* she pushed herself to make the move.

Catching her fingers to stop them, he pushed her back so he could look her in the eye. His breath heaved in and out, his lips trying to form the words. Finally, they came; "I'm sorry."

She stared at him in bewilderment, her emotions screeching to a halt. He had just taken her to the highest point on earth. *What the hell is he sorry about?*

He forced himself to continue. "Look. I didn't escape from the Scorpions. I got pinched. About a month ago, we were on a job, and I got separated. Only after they got me, they didn't have anything on me, and I got no record. So they sent me here for drug addiction." He paused, trying to assess her reaction. She blinked at him, her brow wrinkled.

"So," he continued, "I calls up Brett, and I tells him I'd be here for a month and catch up to them when I'm released. He don't takes it well. He thinks I'm giving up our group, telling the Feds what I knows. He says he'll sees me soon."

Shifting nervously, he rubbed his hand across her waist, his voice growing tender. "Then I recognized you, and I gets this idea. I calls Brett and tells him that I found you. I offers to takes you to him, if he won't kills me and he lets me back in the group. He says that's a deal."

Her eyes narrowed, but she didn't move. She could feel the anger boiling inside her, evidenced by the grinding of her teeth.

His voice dropped to a whisper, and he made a small shake with his head, "I didn't lie, baby. You're my fantasy... I..." she could see the lump move in his throat as he swallowed, "I love you."

The emotion in his eyes; the realization he wasn't lying tore a gaping wound through her chest, softening her rage.

Drawing in a ragged breath, he appeared shaken, "And that means I don't wanna hands you over to Brett. So the way I sees it, I gots two choices. I can hands you over anyways, and have to watch what they dos to you. Or I can run and draws him away from you."

Her expression fell blank, "What do you mean by that?"

"I mean, I'm gonna leave. As soon as we're dressed." For emphasis, he bent over, grabbing his briefs and shoving his legs in. Reaching for his pants he put them on as well before he continued. "I'm gonna head out on my bike and calls him up; gives him some story. I never told him where we are, so he don't knows how to find you. As long as I get away from you, you're safe." Bending over, he latched onto his shirt and pulled it over his head.

Becoming conscious he was serious, she felt like she'd been stomped. Angry tears sprang into her eyes and trickled down her cheeks. "The fuck if you are. If you're leaving, you can damn well take me with you!" She panted loudly, her heart in shreds, her mind pulled between the idea of clinging to him and beating the shit out of him.

Seeing her misery, Enrique pulled her against him once more, wrapping her as tightly as he could, longing to console her. They stood for several minutes, his hand woven into her hair and pressing on her scalp, and his whispering voice begged her forgiveness. "I've never been so sorry... about anything in my life," he breathed, "But, you can't come with me, baby. You know what they'll dos if they catch us. Besides, livin' on the run ain't no kinda life. You deserve better than that, and you have a chance here."

Opting for the clinging, Tori allowed herself to cry as she took in his reasons and searched for the errors in his words. She wanted so desperately to keep him, as if her world were spinning out of control once more.

Finally, he pushed her back so he could continue. "You gotta promise me something."

She raised her chin in defiance, tired of promising things to men who broke her heart.

"You gotta promise me you'll go on. You makes a great life for yourself." He searched her eyes for her consent, but could see she wasn't ready to agree with him.

"I'll gives you my number," he reached into his pocket and produced his small cell. "If anything ever happens, if you ever needs me, you calls me and I'll comes to you. But you gotta swear to me you'll make a real life for yourself." He wished he could promise her more, but didn't dare feed her another lie.

Enrique knew her story. He had come into the Scorpions after the plan had been formed, but he had heard how the

Dragons had taken her and molded her. He had been with the Scorpions when Eddie had arrived to show off his new toy, fifteen years in the making. He knew who she was and what she could do. Brett knew these things, too.

That's why I have to do this; I can't gives her to them. Otherwise, Brett would take her and make her his own, the same as Eddie had done, and her life would be what it had always been. Enrique didn't want that for her, even if it meant he had to let her go. *Yeah,* he debated with himself for a moment, *I loves her that much,* and he consoled himself with a shake of his head, *son of a bitch! I never saw it comin... but this way, at least she gets a chance.*

He stroked her hair for a few more seconds, then turned to the desk and grabbed a small pink piece of paper. Scribbling down the number, he squeezed it into her hand, "Don't lose it, baby girl. Put it in your wallet. Remember: calls me if you haves to, but only if you haves to." Pulling her close one last time, he grazed her lips and pressed his cheek against hers, then grabbed his boots and headed out the door, leaving her standing naked in the tiny room alone.

Rock Bottom

Tori sat on the wooden chair and cried for a while after he left her. Eventually, her tears were spent, and she dressed in slow motion. Picking up the pink piece of paper, she stared at the number, then folded it in half and placed it in her wallet. Leaving the safety of the tiny office, she made her way over to the bar to have another triple before she left. Trudging along, she covered the distance to the tall structure in time.

Enrique had already been by, taking his stuff and moving on. Of course, Brandon had called it in as soon as he realized he had no intention of returning, and a bit of commotion still went on at the house, which allowed her to slip by unnoticed in her inebriated state. Making it to her room, she closed the door and collapsed into her corner, not even bothering to undress.

Tori got up to shut off the alarm at 5:00 am, but lacked the energy to go down for her run. Instead, she went straight to the shower and stood in the warm water for longer than she should have. Beneath the cascade, she thought about all the things that had happened between Enrique and herself in the short time he had been there.

While she allowed the water to soak her, she considered not even putting the makeup on her face, hoping the scar that crossed her eye would keep the world away. She felt tired, like every drop of life had been drained from her by the losses she had faced.

Slowly, Tori forced herself to go through the motions of applying her cover and getting dressed. Going down stairs, she did not stop to eat or speak to anyone, had anyone been there; she really didn't notice or care. Heading out the door, she made her way to work, where she again required herself to go through the motions.

Leaving work that afternoon, she went over to the bar and drank until she couldn't stand up. Then, taking a chair over in a corner, she leaned against the wall and passed out.

Sometime later, she was jarred awake by the sound of loud, boisterous laughter and familiar voices. Sitting up straight, she could make out the faces of Derrick, Max, and Keith. Her heart began to pound out of control when she recognized the girl with them; Lindsey.

Standing groggily, she bumbled over to the pool table where they were making a ruckus and demanded what they were doing there. All four of them obviously had been drinking. The three boys laughed at her, telling her they were not at work, and none of her business what they did. She made eye contact with Lins, who looked away guiltily.

Tori, being pretty wasted herself, decided to sit it out and see what became of it. Stomping back to the bar, she took a stool and asked for water. She had been coming there for enough days to know it was not a hangout for young people. It was a dark place thugs would frequent, and her four young friends might find far more than easy liquor if they were not careful.

Sitting on her stool, drinking her water, she began to sober up, as she watched the group enjoying their beverages and playing at the pool table. She noticed that some of the men nearby were beginning to take an interest in the pretty young blonde in the short skirt. The boys who were with her would be of little use if she needed defending. Tori continued to drink the liquid, swinging her legs lightly on the tall seat.

At some point, another patron leaned a pool cue against the bar close to her, and she reached over, grasping the maple stick in her hands. A good weight, she held it playfully, looking as if she were considering joining the game. Eyeing the group of men off to the side, the six of them were growing more obnoxious with their comments toward her housemate, and were laughing loud enough to be heard over the constant thump of the jukebox that sat to her right along the wall. Remembering her knife tucked in her boot, she hoped she wouldn't need it.

Soon, Tori could almost feel the tick of the clock, and realized midnight had snuck up on them; they had missed curfew. Sitting, watching Lins, she knew it didn't matter. These were her friends, and she would stay and look after them if she had to.

The party rolled on for over an hour more, the three young boys beginning to touch Lins in places they shouldn't have, encouraging her to go home with the three of them for more fun at their place. She refused coyly, giggling at the same time. Tori rubbed the stick between her hands, and then gripped it as if she were choking it. At that moment, the six onlookers made their move.

Three of the men each grabbed a boy, immobilizing them by pinning their arms and forcing them to sit in a chair. Laughing loudly, the leader of the group announced he wanted to give the younger men a proper lesson on how to treat a lady. Turning, he slapped Lindsey across the face.

The girl fell, sprawling crossways on the pool table, her white panties exposed beneath her short skirt. Dazed, the girl struggled to sit up, to no avail, as one of the men leapt onto the table, and knelt beside her to hold her in place.

Tori rose from her seat and in a quick motion, kicked the plug out of the wall and the room fell silent for a moment as the sound from the jukebox came to a sudden halt. She appeared eerily calm as she choked the pool cue, nodding to the men who had made their intentions clear.

The leader of the group had already unbuckled his belt, and glared at the dark haired woman as she stood watching him. Calmly, he reached over and grasped the panties of her young friend, pushing them aside to plunge his finger into her soft folds.

Lins screamed, trying to push his hand away, but drunk and in no condition to put up a fight.

Pulling the digit out, he sucked her juices off, then pointed it at Tori and spoke brusquely, "You best stay outta dis, 'less you want some, too."

Her smile slow and wide, she replied, "Well, I thought you would never ask."

For a moment, the group of men held looks of bright eyed surprise, before the realization of her intent.

Lunging forward, Tori swung the cue in a short arc, catching the one crouched on the slate upside the head, knocking him clear and off onto the floor. Spinning the stick on through and back into position, she jabbed at the leader, working him across the table.

The third quickly dashed around the other side, wanting to grab her and subdue her, but Tori prepared for his assault. Her reflexes were swift, her movements strong and sure. As quickly as the third rounded the corner, she spun herself, catching him in the throat with the stick, not stopping to watch as he fell to his knees, gasping for his life.

This is what the Dragons had trained her for. This was her secret job; the one only dead men knew. Using the cue as if it were a part of her, Tori worked the three over, throwing in punches and kicks with elbows and knees whenever necessary.

Realizing their friends were in trouble, the three who were holding the rest of the group into their seats released them to rush into the fray, only to regret the move almost as quickly.

Catching one of them in the face, Tori sent blood and teeth spewing across the table, staining the green felt. Lindsey, regaining her presence of mind at the gruesome sight, rolled off the other side and huddled with the boys, who watched as if they were made of rocks.

The fight only lasted a minute, as Tori released her anger and the adrenaline flowed. She did not want to kill them, but she would if she had to. The leader stubborn, and not wanting to give up, came for her again. She had the forethought to slip her hand into her boot for her knife when she had the chance.

Recognizing he had charged at her once more, Tori raised her right hand high, the pop of the blade echoing loudly in the small space. Hearing it and seeing the flash of the steel, the brute stopped dead, still staring at her. She dropped the bloody stick and gave him a toothy sneer, her blue eyes dancing with excitement.

Using her left hand to curl her fingers in front of her, she beckoned to him. He flicked his eyes from the blade to her face, then back again, shifting slightly as he considered his chances. Deciding he didn't like the odds, he spit in her direction, telling her to take her friends and go.

Tori wasted no time, rounding the table in a flash, grabbing Max by the collar of his shirt and shoving him towards the door. "Move!" she commanded, taking Lindsey by the arm and half pushing half dragging as they made their way out into the chill night air. "We need to go, *now*!" she stated gruffly. "Where do you guys live?" The three boys shared an apartment a few blocks away, and the five of them made it there faster than one would have expected.

Tori peered around and behind as they scampered along, keeping watch for anyone who would be following or looking for retribution. Once they were inside the small dwelling, everyone fell onto chairs or the floor, panting for air. It was a miracle they had survived.

Looking down at her trembling fingers, Tori could feel her heart pounding inside her chest. Her skills had never mattered as much as they had that night. Clenching her fist repeatedly, she knew the time had come for her to do what she should have done long ago.

"You guys got a phone?" she asked the three boys as they lay gasping. Keith stood and handed her his cell, and she dialed the number to the house. At nearly 2:00 am, she thought she would be waking them.

The phone answered on the first ring, she realized the couple never went to bed until everyone had made it home. Tears touched her eyes as she told Brandon they were ok, and gave him the address where they could be located. She ended by asking him to send the police, and then hung up the phone.

"The police?" Derrick shrieked, "Are you crazy? Why the hell would you want them to send the police?" He stared at her incredulously.

"Because it's the right thing to do." Her reply even toned, she stood waiting for what was to come.

The group sat in silence, no one bothering to ask questions or make commentary. When the police arrived, she handed the officer her knife, and he cuffed her as they read her rights. The kids were all taken to the hospital to be examined, and Tori rode in the back of the car calmly.

Arriving at the station, they booked her for assault and took her to a holding cell, where she waited amongst the others who had been arrested that night. All of the flat surfaces were taken, and many were sprawled on the floor. Tori leaned into a corner of the room and fell asleep. The noise in the hold rose and fell as people were brought in, but it did not disturb her rest. She awoke some hours later, feeling mildly refreshed.

The following day, a short round man in a blue uniform led her to a small room. He asked her to sit at a table that faced a wall made mostly of mirrored glass, and advised her he needed to take her statement about the night's events.

Tori stared at her hands, thinking about how and why she had been in the bar to begin with. Her mind had been turning over the events of her life, especially the ones since she had arrived in LA. Running her fingers through her hair, she said nothing; he wasn't the man she needed to talk to.

Staring at the mirror over his shoulder, she considered if anyone were on the other side. She wondered if anyone would really care what she had to say. Gazing at her reflection, she gave a small smile and waved. Laying her head down on the table, she closed her eyes and waited. A few minutes later, the door opened, and Special Agent James Godfry came into the room.

Presenting his ID, the agent dismissed the officer, and took his seat. "How did you know I was in there?" he asked as he made himself comfortable.

"Just a hunch," she replied breathlessly, lifting her face to smile at him. "Fine mess I've made here, don't you think?"

He chuckled at her insightfulness, "Would you care to explain?"

Tori nodded, knowing in her heart it would be the right thing to do. She began with the flight into town and worked her way forward, recounting every detail she could remember.

Godfry listened, allowing her to share the things she needed to get off her chest. It took a few hours, and they took a short break to allow her to go to the bathroom and get water after a while. Tori left out no fact, even telling him how to find the pistol taped under her nightstand.

When she finished, he inquired, "So, why did you do all of these things? I mean, what were you thinking about?"

Her reply surprised him, "I'm an alcoholic; that's why it happened. Even when I'm sober, my mind is looking for the next time or reason I'll have to drink. If I don't have a reason, then I feel I need to create one; or get myself into one."

Drawing a deep breath, she exhaled slowly, and he waited for her to continue. "I also know, I need to go to prison," she admitted softly, and his eyebrow shot up at the response. "That's the only way everyone will be safe," she elaborated.

Thinking back to her explanation of The Organization, Jim completed the connection to the predator insects from her story. "You meant those quite literally. The Dragons and the Scorpions, and what was it, the Spiders?" his voice remained flat like a statement. Tori nodded, and the two sat in silence as he considered what this meant now, and to the investigation currently under way.

Presently, he continued, "Well, you aren't going to prison. You aren't even going to be prosecuted for what happened at the bar last night." Seeing her about to disagree, he raised his index finger to cut her off, "Not because of our agreement, but because of the circumstances. Not to mention the embarrassment of the guys when they were picked up and told they got the shit kicked out of them by a fifteen year old girl."

"I'm not fifteen," she stated with less conviction than normal. Tori suddenly felt as if she were a puppet on a string. In the past, the Dragons made her dance. Today, the FBI ran the show. Staring across the table at him, she wondered what tune they were going to play next, and what their purpose could be. Calmly, she stated aloud, "I bet Warren is going nuts right about now."

Behind the glass, La Buff's jaw dropped, as he had been

fuming since Jim had left him. Back at the table, Jim felt equally surprised, "What makes you think Agent La Buff is with me?" He tried to sound unaffected, but her intuition had started to scare him.

Tori's smile tickled the corners of her lips, "Just a hunch. So, where's Eli?"

Godfry stared at her for several minutes, tapping his fingers against the tabletop while deciding how to play it. Special Agent Eli Founder had made a very stupid move taking the girl to bed with him. It had not taken long for them to figure out that he had done so, and even worse, Debra Paisley had gotten caught up in the meltdown, and also came under fire. But, as the agency still valued the girl, he had to handle the situation carefully.

Having made up his mind, he spoke slowly to avoid becoming emotional. "Special Agent Founder has been reassigned. I'm not at liberty to give you any details. All I can say is, you have more important work and things to worry about."

Tori raised an eyebrow at his choice of words, considering what work she had to do. She tilted her head slightly, breathing deeply until she realized she would get no answers, and let it go.

Their conversation ended soon after, and she followed him to the front to pick up her things. Taking the jacket as he offered it to her, she managed a weak smile. "Be good," he told her. Turning, he shook Terry's hand.

Tori watched, obediently, somewhat surprised that Terry and not Brandon had been waiting for her. Exiting the building together, she asked if he were going to give her a ride home. Smiling at her across the top of his car as they climbed inside, he said that he was, in a manner of speaking.

They soon pulled up in front of the halfway house; he shut off the engine, and they both went inside. Brandon and

Sharon were waiting for them, and they went into the living room so the four of them could sit down. Terry had, in fact, brought her to collect her things, as it had been agreed she would not be allowed back at the house. Sharon sat watching the girl, and she noticed her fidgeting with her fingers, and her heart went out to her.

With a wave of her hand, Sharon interrupted her husband as he explained their decision to remove her, and stated quietly, "Jim tells me you've decided you're an alcoholic. Can you tell me why that is?"

The question surprised Tori, as she had not realized he would share what she told him with anyone. Pausing to consider the question, she tried to think how to answer in a short but honest way.

"Because I feel like I'm at the bottom of a deep dark well. Rock bottom. It doesn't matter what happens to me, all I think about is having a drink..." the girl paused, leaving out her other urges. "Today's reasons; yesterday's... they don't really matter. All I want is the tingle and the numb that will follow. It's a feeling I can't fight, and just the smell of it makes my mouth water; and it's the vilest liquid I have ever tasted."

Tori drew a deep breath and exhaled it slowly. She expected that to be enough, but everyone sat quietly and waited for her to continue, so she did.

"When I have a drink, I don't have just one. I have a triple. Three triples. I drink until I can't see, or walk, until I lose consciousness. Maybe I'm wrong, but I don't think that I'm normal; I don't think the sight of a liquor store should make your hands shake." Pausing for a moment, she swallowed hard at her own revelations. "I used to go to those meetings, those AA meetings and think those people were foolish, and I was nothing like them. I didn't need their help, or anyone's help."

Sharon smiled. She had heard those words from many people, including her own self. "What do you need, Tori?"

Their girl's voice grew small, on the verge of tears. Blinking rapidly, she tried not to let them fall. "I can't do this by myself. I don't know who's going to help me, but I know I'll never make it alone. I tried to get them to send me to prison, where I wouldn't have a choice. You know, like when I was in the hospital. It was easy when there wasn't any way to get a bottle. But now, it's like I'm going to find a way to get it. Even though I know I shouldn't, I keep doing things, and I can't stop." She had reached the end, and they weren't going to make her go any further.

Standing, Tori went up the stairs, the tears dripping onto her shirt, making small color rings as she walked. Pulling her suitcase out from under the bed, she began to place her clothes inside of it. Folding the long sleeved shirts, she thought about how she always tried to cover her scars, hoping to be what people wanted her to be; trying to be normal.

Why can't I just be who I am? She asked herself the question, and answered it in the next breath; *because who I am doesn't fit in this world,* and for a moment she wished Enrique had taken her to the Scorpions. At least they would have accepted her and not made her feel like she was wrong to be herself.

Hearing a noise, she looked up to find Sharon standing at her door. "We need you downstairs, please. Wash your face and join us."

Wash my face? Tori stared blankly at the request. Stepping into the bathroom, she could see the large patches of her makeup that were streaked and distorted. Using the soap, she leaned over the sink and washed it clean away and dried her tired skin, then trudged back down to rejoin the others.

Tori arrived back in the living room, her long hair hiding her face. They had all been warned about her scar, but none of them had seen it. Lifting her head and pulling her long tresses to the side, she watched their reactions, waiting for their expressions to change or for them to comment. Terry smiled and indicated she should sit down. She didn't know which she disliked more, having people react to her scar, or the fact that they ignored it.

Taking her seat next to him, she braced herself for whatever they were going to say. Listening, they began to go over the new rules she would be held to, which included daily Breathalyzer tests. She would also not be allowed to go anywhere without supervision until further notice. And finally, she would not be permitted to have sex or any type of physical contact other than platonic; *damn, they know you're a filthy whore as well as a drunk.*

Listening patiently, it dawned on her that they were talking about new rules because she would be remaining in the house, after all. Blinking rapidly, she stopped them to clarify the point, "You're gonna let me stay here? And I still get to work at the music store?"

Nodding, Sharon turned both palms to the ceiling, smiling brightly. Tori reached over and grabbed Terry around the neck, hugging him tightly. She felt so grateful to the three of them, she wasn't sure she would ever be able to express it, or repay it.

A New Leaf

Tori sat in amazed silence, staring at the suitcase on her bed. Only a few hours ago, she had been packing it to leave. Now, she would unpack it, being allowed to stay. More than that, Sharon and Lins were going to take her shopping. Thinking back to the first and only girly day and shopping spree she had ever been on, the one with Debra Paisley when she bought her current wardrobe, she began to feel nervous.

She didn't worry about being around women anymore; she had gotten over that. She wasn't anxious about people seeing the scar on her face; she had grown tired of caring about what other people thought. Mostly, she felt concerned about doing the right thing. She wanted to make the people who cared about her proud.

Tori's mind lazily pondered the advice Terry had given her. He said to take one step at a time, and not to worry when she felt bad or if she messed up. There were going to be lots of people looking out for her, because they cared about her. She was turning over a new leaf, and that would take time to grow and nurture.

At that moment, Lindsey's short, thin frame appeared at the door. Looking up, Tori saw for the first time the large shiner she sported on her left eye, and could not hide her surprise. "Is that from last night?" she stammered.

The girl came in and bounced on her bed, "Yup," she replied brightly. "But thanks to you, that's the worst of it." Her smile lessening a bit, she went on, "I really owe you a lot, you know. I mean, things could have been really bad or would have been, if you hadn't been there to stand up for me. Thank you."

Tori felt touched by her warm words, not really expecting her gratitude.

"So," Lins continued with an excited grin, "Tomorrow we go shopping to get you some new clothes."

"Now, you can wait right there," Tori cut in while holding up her hand, "I'll go shopping with you and I'll get some new clothes, but I can already assure you they're going to look like the clothes I already have. Minus the sleeves, I think. I like my clothes. I love my clothes."

Lins laughed, shaking the ringlets that framed her round face, "Yeah, yeah, we'll see about that. Come on, let's go downstairs and get dinner."

As if on cue, Tori's stomach growled and she stood up, following the shorter girl out of the room and down to the kitchen. When they came to the door, she felt a slight tingle of nerves in her hands as she awaited the reaction to her face. To her relief, there were some double takes, but everyone took it pretty well and ignored it after that.

To her surprise, Max, Keith, and Derrick were waiting for her in front of the sink. She grinned from ear to ear at the sight of them, and they each came to give her a strong hug and express their gratitude in much the same fashion that Lins had. She tried to blow them off, playfully, but at that moment they really meant a great deal to her.

While they were talking, Tori's mouth began to water at the smells that surrounded her. Looking about, she discovered they had set up a pit in the driveway, where a big rack of steaks would be ready any minute. On the bar sat homemade potato salad, coleslaw, and a salad with lots of different veggies in it. It was a special meal, prepared for a friend.

The meal almost complete, the whole group began taking their seats around the giant dining room table. Once they were seated, the plates were served, and they ate hungrily, each eager to finish for the banana pudding dessert.

Swinging her gaze around the table, Tori basked in the warm feelings she had for this group of people. She had never had a family, but somehow she thought this might be what it would be like, with everyone gathered around a meal to share stories and each other's company. When the food had been consumed, and the pudding was served, she sensed the change as it fell over the room. No one asked. No one even hinted. But they all wanted to know.

Clearing her throat, she thanked everyone for the generosity and their kindness. "I really appreciate you guys," her words came from the bottom of her heart. A murmur of agreement arose, and they waited again.

Staring at her bowl, Tori felt her palms go clammy. "So, is there anything anyone would like to ask me, since I'm in a good mood and might actually tell you the answer?" There, she had laid the offer on the table, so to speak.

Immediately, voices went up around the room, but Max's appeared to be the loudest. "I just wanna know who the hell you are," he said laughing. "I mean, I have to admit you're probably the weirdest person I have ever met, and I mean that in a good way, but you're . . . different I guess." He grinned tentatively, realizing his words might have offended her.

Tori smiled at the boy, at the moment quite open to the idea of telling them where she came from. "That's because, I'm not like you. Any of you. And to be honest, I don't really know who I am." Tori didn't want to share the most gruesome parts, but there were some things that she could give up about herself that would help with her problems; things that were safe for them to know.

"I was raised by a group of men who were not related to me in any way. They were mercenaries who made money by illegal means. They're the ones who educated me, and I never went to school or did ordinary kid stuff."

Derrick laughed, "Yeah, so you were home schooled."

Some chuckled as well, and Tori tried to keep her sense of humor as she continued. "When they thought I was old enough, they forced me into their group, did unspeakable things to me," she pointed at her eye, "And I did things for them that I deeply regret. When I had had enough, I killed them to stop them and gain my freedom."

The room had become graveyard quiet, so she nodded to herself, "And now I'm trying to figure out who I want to be." She shrugged and smiled, and her story ended.

Thinking for a bit, Max still wanted more, and asked, "And they taught you to speak Spanish and Russian?"

Tori lifted her shoulders again, "More or less, I learned naturally because they all spoke multiple languages. I actually also speak French and German. I guess you could say, they taught me a lot of unusual things."

Derrick spoke up again, "You know, your life actually sounds pretty cool. I mean, last night was incredible!" He grinned widely, his admiration sincere.

Growing a little sad, Tori shook her head, "No, it hasn't been cool. It hasn't been cool at all. And last night, I only did what I had to do." *I always do… what I have to do.* Reaching for her water, her expression became somber, and if anyone else had a question, they did not ask.

The party disbursed within the hour, and Tori felt free to return to her room and get ready for bed. Unpacking her suitcase, she put her things back into her chest of drawers. Picking up her jacket, she placed it onto the back of her chair. Opening her wallet, she stared at the pink piece of paper. She reached in to touch it for a moment, then closed the leather pouch and laid it aside.

Thinking about the events of the last twenty-four hours, she wondered if they had actually confiscated her tool kit from her jacket. To her surprise, she found it still inside the inner pocket, but even more shocking, she found the knife there. She pulled it out, staring at it; the thought occurred to her that the Feds were really playing games with her.

Dropping it back into the slot, she went around the bed and kneeled down to feel under the nightstand. Her heart began to pound as she touched the cold steel, still taped underneath. Sitting on her knees, Tori began to tremble, and she wiped her mouth anxiously. Running her hands through her long hair repeatedly, she considered what it all meant.

Eventually, she put on her night clothes and curled up in her corner to sleep. Sitting there, with her face against the wall, she thought to herself wryly, *someday you're gonna have to learn to sleep in the bed.* Eli Founder had tried to get her to, by putting her bed into the corner back in the mental ward of the hospital. In the end, she had squatted on the bed to lean in the corner.

Getting up when the alarm went off, Tori slipped into her workout gear and made her way downstairs. Running towards the playground, she thought about her new house rules that had been added, and wondered if she should be supervised at the moment. The thought of one of them getting up at 5:00 am to run with her made her laugh out loud.

Arriving at the school, her heart leapt into her throat when she made out the outline of a man, leaning on the bars she had been using to exercise. Stopping short of the grass, she stared at the figure, her chest pounding, as she comprehended she could be in danger.

The shadow noticed her, raising a hand to wave. Tori took a step back, and the figure began to jog over to her, nursing a slight limp. Holding her ground, she waited.

Terry came running up, a wide grin on his face. "Did I scare you?"

Tori began to laugh at her fear, her voice vibrating with relief. "What the fuck are you doing here, old man?" she demanded in a joking tone. *And how he had known I use this spot?* She didn't bother to ask.

Spreading his hands wide, he proclaimed, "Supervising," as if it should have been perfectly obvious.

She wasn't sure if he acted as the trainer, or if she did, but together, they worked through exercises and routines, and she never exercised alone again. It turned out to be great fun, because they pushed each other hard, exactly as she and Brian had done back in the day. However, she never forgot that moment of terror, and always wondered how much he came to supervise her, and how much he played the role of body guard.

One of the Girls

The three girls set out on their girl's day out first thing after breakfast. Sharon had made some appointments for them in the morning, and they would look for clothes in the afternoon. Tori started to protest, upset she would miss work, but Sharon asserted she had the day off; Terry had insisted. *Funny, he didn't mention it this morning,* she grumbled to herself.

Taking the car, the trio headed over to a salon, where they were given manicures and pedicures. Tori had never experienced either one, and found that someone touching her feet felt very unnerving. Noticing that the other women seemed to be enjoying theirs, she laid her head back and tried to relax. *Come on, you know how to do this. Just breathe.*

She could feel the clippers on her toes as her nails were trimmed, which gave her the incredible urge to pull her foot away, but she made it through. She also felt as if she would hyperventilate when the attendant applied the creamy lotion. Peeking over, Lins giggled at her, and she wished she had something to throw at the girl.

When they were finished, she hoped they were ready to leave, but when they passed through a glass partition, she realized they were moving into the section for cutting hair. Twirling her lengthy locks around her hand, she began backing away, adamant there was no way they were cutting her wavy strands.

Showing her palms in a very non-combative manner,

Sharon tried to reasure her, "They're just gonna trim it and condition it for you, not cut too much off at all."

Pointing at her, Tori demanded, "You gotta promise - no, you gotta *swear;* that's all they're gonna do."

Sharon and Lins both raised their right hands to take the oath. With a sigh and a slight pout, Tori agreed and another attendant escorted her to a chair in front of a large black sink. Cautiously sliding into the seat, she leaned back and rested her neck on the rim.

A woman in a colorful smock massaged her scalp and washed her hair with minty smelling shampoo. This made her begin to feel more at ease than the footwork, and she closed her eyes and inhaled deeply, remembering the times Henry would wash her hair in the stream in Brazil, where she grew up.

Afterwards, the woman put in a deep conditioner, which she also rinsed out. Finally, Tori sat in another chair, her heart pounding as she watched them work in the mirror. A tall curvy woman combed through her long tresses, lifting sections to trim the ends. When the woman finished, Tori observed her ebony locks, noting a bit of bounce, and maybe a little extra sheen, but other than that, they looked the same to her.

Finally, the salon work completed, the time had come to look for clothes. Tori, already feeling exhausted, thought to herself, *I wonder if I will ever like being one of the girls.*

Entering a small boutique, Lins let out a small shriek and made a dash for a set of lacy skirts hanging on and next to a mannequin. Upon seeing this, Tori decided the answer to her previous question would be an emphatic *no*; being put off by skirts, lace and shrieking.

Turning away, she marched across the store, picking her way through racks of hanging garments. On the wall, there were tee shirts folded neatly on shelves. Looking across the rows, she saw many colors, solid and striped. Making her way down, she lifted a few, holding them up to her body, and then dropped them back onto the piles. The last row was white. Finding the extra larges that fit her shoulders best, she counted out five and picked them up.

Watching with mild concern, Sharon suggested the girl try one other color, or maybe some tank tops.

Trying to be accommodating, Tori looked at the tank tops, then decided against them on account of her Dragon mark would show. She still could not shake the feeling of being vulnerable, and the idea that some unsavory person would recognize it made her reluctant to wear them.

Walking calmly down the row a second time, she finally did choose a second color: black. Picking up five of those as well, she felt she was done. Turning and giving her newest female friends a smile, she wanted to head for the exit.

However, Sharon led her over to the jean tables, where she had to choose from umpteen different styles and colors in those as well, until she finally decided to get more boot cut blue denim jeans, exactly like the ones she always wore. Sharon and Lins didn't look happy, but Tori grinned from ear to ear as she placed the items on the counter.

Sharon had wanted her to try something new, and actually regretted offering to pay for them since she wasn't changing anything but her sleeves. Later, when she saw the scars on the girl's arms, she realized going sleeveless already meant a big change, and they would have to go for color the next time.

Finally finished, they stopped at a small café for an early dinner, where Tori felt the memory of the afternoon she had spent with Debra brought happily to mind. Sitting down to her meal, she wondered what had become of her first female friend. They had dined at a small outdoor eatery, and Tori had given in to the urge to share part of her story with the woman. She had, therefore, explained what had happened to her, the reason she would never be able to have children. She shuddered at the memory.

Seeing this, Sharon reached over in a motherly fashion and brushed the girl's long hair with her fingers. "Everything ok?" she asked in a soft voice.

Looking up from her lap to see the woman's face, Tori found the gesture comforting, and pondered for a split second what it might have been like to have a mother. "I'm fine," she replied. "Just thinking; wondering what it's like to have a mom."

Lins broke in, exclaiming in an irritated voice, "It depends on the mom. Mine is an example of the worst kind."

Tori stared at her in disbelief. Lins had been talking to her for weeks about her life and how great it had been. She stated calmly, "Well, I guess you'll have to explain what you mean by that then."

Lindsey's mother was only sixteen when she was born, and had been a cheerleader in high school. A pretty girl, she had assumed that Lindsey's father would marry her, which he did. However, it did not take long for him to decide that being a family man was not what he really wanted to do, so he left them soon after he graduated.

Lindsey's mother had dropped out of school after being married, and had not finished. She was still a pretty girl and decided it would be easier to find a man who would take care of them than it would be to go back to school, or to work too hard herself. Lindsey was two when the parade of men started.

In seven years, her mother had dated several dozen prospective candidates. Several of them had been abusive, both to her mother, and to Lins herself. However, only after she came down with *Trichomoniasis*, an STD, had anything been done about her situation. She was nine at the time.

Taken from her mother, Lins went to live with her grandparents, who were mortified by their daughter's behavior. To compensate, they gave the girl whatever she wanted. By the time she herself was in high school, she was very sexually active, had a raging drug and alcohol problem, and had even had a miscarriage at the age of fifteen.

"And that's how I ended up in a halfway house, at the age of eighteen," she finished with a hint of anger in her voice. "After having spent a month in a residential treatment facility again earlier this year, my grandparents have finally given up on me, I guess."

"And you blame your mom," Tori's words came tumbling out before she had considered how they might sound.

Lins stared at her in a state of confusion, turning a palm to the sky, "Who else would I blame?"

Tori leaned forward, resting her forearms on the table. Taking a deep breath, she realized she had started a conversation she regretted.

"Well, don't get me wrong," she tried to repair the damage. "I understand that your mother allowed people to do terrible things to you, and those things can never be undone. But at some point, you have to stand up and say, ok, from here on, this part is mine. It is and will be what I make it. That's exactly where I am right now, trying to make this part mine." Deep down, Tori only hoped there would be no more interference from her past in the process.

Lindsey stared at her for a moment, coming to realize their stories were very similar. "You said last night you weren't like any of us. But you were wrong!" she accused with a frown.

Tori quickly quipped an agreement, having come to the same conclusion, "Yeah, I see that; you and I have a lot in common, now that I have heard your real story. More than I ever thought could be possible." She wrinkled her nose at the pretty blonde, "But, you never mentioned any of that stuff when we talked before. All *you* ever said was how great your life is and all the things you have gotten to do." She ended in a slightly accusatory tone, not really sure if she was right to feel she had been lied to.

Lins nodded, "Of course," the girl wafted her hand, "I don't go around telling people about all the bad stuff unless I really know them and can trust them. I focus on the good things around me and in my life. It helps me keep a positive attitude. Besides, it's embarrassing to tell people you got an STD when you were nine years old because your mother's boyfriend couldn't keep his hands off; like it's your fault somehow that some perverted bastard was touching you."

Leaning back, Tori's mind raced. She had learned some very valuable lessons that day. *When looking at people, I should look for the similarities instead of the differences.* She also understood why Lins felt the need to keep people from knowing the truth; for the same reason she covered her own scars. She knew that made them even more connected.

Tori made a promise to herself; like her friend, she would be mindful to look at the good things around her more often, and accept the things she could not change. She felt guilty as she remembered where she had heard that before. Taking a deep breath, she contemplated the idea, *maybe I might like to be one of the girls after all.*

Down the Road

The next day, Tori got ready for her return to work. For the first time, she would wear one of her new white shirts, with the short sleeves. Her scarred face remained covered, but her arms showed. What's worse, she noticed that the V neck on the tees left her cleavage exposed, and therefore her bite mark on her left breast became visible at the right angle. She started to put on the long-sleeved that covered everything, but she had grown tired of wearing them, as they were constrictive and overly warm.

Instead, she rapped lightly on Lins' door. *It's time for another woman's opinion,* she decided. The petite blonde responded after a few tries, and instantly Tori could tell she was not a morning person. She found herself laughing at the cute bed-head style the girl wore, and the robe that wrapped crookedly around her tiny frame.

"What do you want?" Lins demanded. "You have any idea what time it is?"

"Yeah, it's seven," Tori laughed again, having been up for a couple of hours. "I need your help." Lins crinkled her forehead at her new friend, but stepped aside. Sitting on the edge of the bed to improve the view, the woman said bluntly, "See my cleavage?"

Lins scowled, "Is that a trick question?" Tori shook her head no, so the girl leaned over to peek down, and realized she meant the scar. "Oh," she murmured, "Can't you put makeup on it? Like your face?"

Tori jumped up as if she had been shocked by a bolt of lightning. Grabbing the other girl for a quick hug, she called, "You're the best!" as she left the room.

"That's all you wanted?" Lins shouted after her, shutting the door heavily and flopping back onto the bed.

Back in her bathroom, Tori lifted her shirt over her head and inspected her breast. She opened the bottle of cover and applied a small amount to the bite mark. Of course, she then realized that the flesh on her chest did not match that on her face, so the spot of makeup showed up really well against her milky white skin. However, the teeth marks were not showing through, and in the end a dark spot would draw less attention than the alternative.

Pulling her shirt back over her head, she realized that this would be a good temporary fix. Leaning over so she could see down her shirt in the mirror, she grinned, very pleased with the results. She washed her hands and switched off the light on her way out, her hair bouncing as she walked. She stopped at the fridge for her customary water and fruit breakfast, and then took a seat at the small bar.

Richard had risen early that morning, and sat at the large dining table they had feasted at the night before last. Giving him a half smile, she noticed he had a very large book in front of him. Thinking back to the collection she had once owned, a small sigh escaped her glossed lips.

Almost instantly, she remembered Lins' advice about not dwelling on the sad things she could not change. Tori switched her thoughts to something more positive, and went over the things she had learned so far at the store.

This brought a smile to her features in an instant. Terry had been diligent about giving her new skills she would be able to use down the road. He had taught her about several aspects of running a business, such as paying the bills and handling the cash. She still had a lot to learn though.

Glancing up at the clock, it read 7:30, and she needed to be on her way. Giving Richard a friendly smile and "See you later," she picked up the frosty water bottle and headed out the back of the house.

It took her the customary twenty minutes to make her way to the store, where she let herself in and locked the door behind her. Inside, she went to the office to count the tills from the previous day and fill out the paperwork to verify they were correct. Placing the deposit in the safe at 8:15, she realized she had gotten really fast at completing it, and might not need to come in so early.

Out on the sales floor, she walked around to inspect the fixtures to see that everything was in order before opening. Rounding the room, she passed the small stage area and came up to the glass counter next to it. Looking up at the row of custom electric guitars, her mind clicked on the idea and her heart began to race.

Pulling the ring out of her pocket, her fingers trembled as she fitted the key into the lock. Taking down a glossy white instrument, Tori breathed in short quick spasms of excitement. She had learned how they worked through helping customers and selling requirements, but she had not actually tried to play one herself.

She had learned to play Henry's acoustic when they lived in Brazil, and she always felt a stab of loss when she thought about him and the times she had shared with him as a child, strumming and singing in the afternoons.

Her mind sinking into the past as she held her new toy, Tori remembered how large the neck had felt when she learned to play. Her hand had barely been big enough to reach around and grasp the frets properly. Henry had been so patient with her, as he always had been; he had instructed her to keep her fingers arched and only press one string at a time with the end of her small digits. Her heart continued to pound as she picked up a standard cord and took the guitar over to the amp beside the small stage area.

First, Tori plugged one lead into the guitar, her palms tingling as it snapped into place. She turned the volume down on the instrument, and then reached over to set the volume and gain to zero on the amp. She blew a puff of air onto a few strands of loose hair, pulling them back out of the way. A small smile tickling the corners of her mouth, she snapped the other lead into the input slot on the amp.

She spent the rest of the time adjusting the volume and gain, trying out different sound levels and letting her fingers remember their way up and down the fret board. By the end of the hour, she was hooked. Just as holding Henry's old guitar had been, this made her heart sing, and she planned to pull one down every day from then on if she could.

Returning the cord to the box after powering everything down, Tori hung the guitar back in place on the wall and locked the rack. Giving the instrument an affectionate stroke, she hummed to herself as she went about opening the registers.

Max and Derrick arrived before 10:00 am. Things were much friendlier between them, with smiles and good mornings, and the pair noticed her mood seemed exceptionally bright. She gave them the short list of things that needed to be tackled, and they quickly went to work putting out freight and re-shelving the items that were out of place.

Terry made it in at 11:00 am to take the deposit to the bank. When he returned, he picked up on the lesson over AP. She took to it quickly this time, and he had no trouble explaining how to fill out the payment vouchers and match up the packing slips with the purchase orders and invoices. While she filled in the summary sheet and prepared to complete a check run, she took the opportunity to ask if all businesses worked the same way.

Giving himself a moment to think, Terry adjusted the printer paper tray and placed the blank check forms in, facing the right direction. Nodding, he explained, "The basics are the same, no matter the business. AP is the money going out to pay bills and buy inventory. AR is money coming in from sales. You know," he ended the lesson as the run finished, and placed the blank checks back into the safe, "You should think about taking some classes at one of the colleges here."

"I can't do that," she replied flatly. "I've never been to school anywhere. I already looked it up, and I have to have a high school diploma to even apply." She looked at her lap, a little sad, noticing the scars that ran down her uncovered arms.

"You can," he insisted, his voice growing softer, "You have a GED certificate, or general equivalency diploma." Tori looked up at him from her seated position. He nodded, deciding it was time she knew. "Didn't you ever wonder about all those tests they were giving you back in Chicago?"

She shrugged, turning her left palm up. "I took lots of tests. Who knows what all of them were for?"

"Hmmm; well, then let's go have lunch, shall we?" his voice sounded chipper as he turned to show her out.

They locked the office, leaving the checks on the desk to be stuffed when they returned. Putting Derrick in charge, they made their way down the street to the diner Tori and Max had visited her first day on the job, which seemed like such a long time ago after all that had happened.

Sliding into the booth, she decided to try the pot roast again, having enjoyed it the first time. Terry ordered the same, and they had ice water to drink. Handing the waitress their menus, he shifted in his seat, considering where to begin.

"Remember the first day you came into the shop, and

said I didn't want you there?" Tori nodded her agreement with a brief smile, so he continued, "I never said that it wasn't true, but I should have. I did want you to come to my store. Sure, Jim had to tell me a lot about you to quote, *convince me*, but in the end, I knew this would be a good place for you and I had a lot to offer you." She liked the way he moved his hands when he spoke, adding punctuation to his words.

"Take teaching you about running a business, for example," he elaborated. "Someday, you may want to have a shop of some kind and what I'm giving you is a set of tools that could help you accomplish that goal." He paused, looking at her as she listened intently, thinking how clear and focused she appeared. "It's ok if you don't, but it'll be there if you ever want it."

Tori considered his words for a moment, and he began explaining to her about her performance in Chicago.

"Now, from what Jim explained, they gave you a whole battery of exams, starting with some that were just to see if you could read and write. They tested your math skills and what you knew about science, and so on. They found that you are not a fantastic writer."

Her disappointed look caused him to backpedal, "Not that you can't write, mind you; let's just say it's not your strongest asset. What they found was," he stopped, not sure he could put their findings into the right perspective. "Well, they found that you are really, really smart. So, since you already had a wide range of knowledge, they gave you a set of exams for a GED."

"Your score averaged seven-forty, which is actually very good. It means you have the equivalent of a high school diploma, and that certificate will be yours when you are emancipated. That's what the committee is planning on doing. Then, you'll be able to go to college and learn about whatever career you choose." Stopping there for their meal that had arrived, he decided that he had gone far enough, opting not to tell her about the rest of the exams and save them for a later date.

Tori sat silently considering what she had learned while she ate. Being able to go to college did not impress her. The reason she had looked into it at all was to take some classes in things that interested her, not because she wanted a degree or anything.

However, Terry left her with a feeling that she would be capable of doing whatever she wanted in her future if she put her mind to it, and that being the most important thing. In the end, this gave her a lot to consider, and a better understanding that the path of her life had yet to be decided.

The pair walked back to the store in a comfortable silence. Tori had come to appreciate the older man with his earnest advice and care for her. A smile on her lips as they ambled along, she felt almost content in her new life now that she had truly accepted being in it.

"You know," he said as they covered the last block, "This is a good time to feed your soul. Really put yourself into things that make you feel good."

Tori's mind jumped to the white guitar hanging on the back wall of the store, causing a brief flicker of a smile.

"Build something, grow something," he pulled up short at the doors, "Learn something new. Enjoy your life, Tori. I have a place I would like to take you on Sunday morning, if you want to go. I'm sure you have never been, and I have an old friend I think it's time you met."

Terry never opened the store on Sundays. He liked to keep the day for doing recreational activities. He also enjoyed the shop being quiet so he could work in the back on building the custom guitars in peace. Tori had spent the first few Sunday afternoons there in the workshop with him, learning the process, but he took this opportunity to encourage her to branch out, try other things that nurtured her inner being.

His offer mysterious, she eyed him curiously, knowing Jim was an old friend, but she already knew him. With a shy smile, she agreed to the outing.

Terry showed a bit more of his teeth and told her he would pick her up at the house on Sunday then, at 9:30 am, and to wear something clean; whatever she had that was the nicest.

Tori only owned two types of outfits; workout clothes and jeans with tees. *And of course sleeping attire,* she had to laugh at the thought, *I wonder which type would qualify as… the nicest.*

All My Sins

The remainder of the week passed smoothly as Tori's new routine had been designed to give her a great deal of support. She rarely spent time alone, unless she opened the store before the rest of the employees arrived. During those times she rushed to get her work done so she could have a few minutes to play with her new shiny friend.

She loved the way the guitar felt in her hands and the variety of sounds she could make with it. She took the songs Henry had taught her long ago and played them in new ways. She had never learned to read music, and really didn't care to, having a particular talent for reproducing what she heard. Her confidence grew, and she began to branch out, listening to a variety of music and artists on the PA during the day, then recreating what she heard when she played.

Tori wasn't really hiding the fact that she did this; she just never mentioned it to anyone. She made sure to put everything back in its place before anyone arrived. It became her private time to feed her soul, being one of the few secrets she allowed herself to keep, as she had learned the hard way that keeping things from the people who cared about her could be dangerous for her.

Sunday morning came, and Tori put on a clean pair of her new jeans and one of the black tees. Since she still did not know where they were going, she made a strong effort to do as he had requested, taking extra care with her grooming of hair and makeup. Applying the cover to her scarred breast, she thought about ways that she might cover it that would be permanent.

Tori knew she could probably get a tattoo that would conceal the eyesore, not sure she wanted to do that on such a tender part of her body. Not to mention, it would have to be a design she could stand to look at for the rest of her life. For the time being, the makeup worked, and if anyone ever noticed, no one had mentioned it.

Terry came in through the kitchen entrance at precisely 9:30. Tori sat at the low bar sipping water and talking to Richard about motorcycles. He had become interested in them since she had been in the house, and it fascinated him how much she knew. That particular morning, he had looked up obscure facts about them and tried to stump her, to no avail.

Terry smiled at them, happy to see her building positive relationships; "Are you ready?"

Tori nodded, standing to leave. Walking out to his small car, she asked, "So, am I allowed to know where we're going yet?" He wore a pair of dress pants and a pressed shirt, and it made her a little edgy that he looked so fancy.

Terry held up his hand in a stopping motion, "You can wait a few minutes more."

Fifteen blocks later, they pulled up in front of a small white building with a tall point on the roof. Tori swallowed hard as she looked up at it, realizing she had been inside a church only one other time in her life, and it made her cringe at the thought of what they had done there.

The Dragons had rolled into a small town just before a huge storm hit. Seeing the lightening cracking the sky, Eddie had started looking for a place for them to crash for the night. Almost all of the houses had lights on inside, so it looked pretty grim, when they saw a small white structure with a playground beside it off in the distance.

The group rode past it, looping around to hide their bikes on the back side. Kicking in a stained glass window, partially hidden by a bush, one of them scurried inside to open the door and let the others in.

They made it inside moments before the rains came, and it appeared the storm would last a while. Having a look around, they discovered a small pantry that had snacks in it, like graham crackers and such, which must have been for children, as the room next door had tiny furniture in it.

Some of the guys ate what they found, and Tori located a partial bottle of Rum in Paul's pack. He let her have some, but it wasn't nearly enough to put her out for the night, which meant she would be awake to endure what was to follow. However, practiced at being convincing when playing her part, she could do it sober if she had to.

Eventually, the group settled in a room that had a few pieces of furniture in it, like a small lounge, with a long sofa and a couple of stuffed chairs. Tori immediately took off her clothes, not wanting them to be soiled or torn by the grasping hands that would soon be upon her.

Many of the guys enjoyed watching her undress. Like she did so often, she made a show out of it, swinging her hips as she worked her jeans down. Moving slowly and rubbing her hands over her bare skin, she removed her bra and lacy panties.

By the time she was naked, her lips were tingling from the liquor. She felt thankful for even that small amount, as it allowed her to take on her role easily, good at playing her part.

David grew anxious, driven by his need for attention, so he pulled his manhood out, and sat on the couch. The position exposed his hardened desire, which stood straight up in front of him. She could hear the crack and roll of thunder when her gaze fell upon him.

Using a finger to motion her over, he grinned widely as she knelt down in front of him and began to work on his swollen need. Grasping him firmly with her right hand, she licked him thoroughly, taking him into her mouth and down her throat, and then sliding him out again to tease him with her fingers.

While Tori busied herself with David, Paul came up behind her and prepared her for the night. She knew that in the cooped up space with the storm outside, there would be nothing for anyone to do, but fuck, and she was ready to take the lot of them if need be.

She tried to focus on what her lips and tongue were doing as she felt Paul push his way inside her. She could feel him slapping against her wet folds that covered her soft hollow as he grabbed her hips and worked himself against her.

David stroked her hair as she did her best to please him, not aware he enjoyed his view of what took place behind her as much, if not more than, anything she did to him. He could see Paul moving in and out in quick stabbing motions, and the combination of the two events put a completely satisfied smirk on his face.

Paul only lasted a few minutes, and Tori could feel his deposit squirt out of her when he withdrew, then the thick fluid that oozed down her leg. She panted heavily, only a moment's break, as the rest of those who intended to have a turn at her were ready in quick succession.

Tori grasped at David's throbbing organ, continuing to concentrate on the distraction. She began to feel tired as the number grew, with only some of them bothering to reapply the gel that made them slide more easily inside her. Maintaining her façade of acceptance, she did her best to prevent any negative thoughts or feelings from reaching the surface and being exposed, having learned long ago what they expected of her.

This became quite a challenge for her when Red came up for his turn. He slapped her across her butt cheeks several times, and then grabbed her roughly as he shoved his shaft inside her. Tori gasped for air; her lungs clamped down with the spasms that rocked her entire body.

David continued to stroke her head, her cheek pressed against his bare thigh, and a bit of drool dripping onto his flesh. With Tori unable to continue, he took over and began to stroke himself, his left hand still massaging her scalp and pulling at her hair at the same time.

Red took the time to abuse her breasts in his typical, grasping manner. Desperately, Tori tried to hang on, confident Red would be the last, as he often was. He noticed how David fed on his actions, and he grabbed a fist full of ebony strands to tug her against him more firmly.

Pulling her up, he cursed her loudly for good measure, "Nasty fucking bitch... Filthy slut... Fucking cunt." He did not seem to have a particular favorite, and would switch them around randomly as he slighted her. Accustomed to the practice, she appeared unmoved by his insulting tirade; all part of the game he loved to play.

Red drove her hard, and when David couldn't hold back any longer, he released onto her face and chest where Red held her. Thankfully, seeing this put Red over the edge as well, and he pulsed inside her as he pushed her forward, her face lying against the other man's lap while he deflated. She allowed a small sigh of relief, confident she had completed the night and would be able to rest.

She lay panting for several minutes, relaxing and focused on holding her blank expression perfectly. David leveraged his way up and over her, finished with her like an old pair of shoes. She lay with her jaw constrained against the cushions of the couch, small amounts of goo trickling out of her and sliding down her legs as she contemplated where she would sleep for the night.

Before she had made up her mind, she felt a hand slide up her thigh, squeezing her butt cheek, and then the other being grasped to spread her. Someone pushed his way inside, and she recognized Eddie without even peeking.

Eddie was Red's identical twin brother, and she exhaled slowly as she prepared for his brand of torture.

The man took her slowly, rubbing her back and sides with his large hands. He had begun to treat her with great tenderness, so to speak, since they had been on the road, playing Dr. Jekyll to Red's Mr. Hyde. Reaching to grasp her sore chest, he lifted her up and pulled her back against him as he remained on his knees, gravity forcing her body down upon him.

Eddie whispered softly in her ear, using sweet and loving pet names for her. She could feel his hands as they slid over the fresh welts and scratches Red had left, his touch burning while he moved to soothe her. In reality, being with him and his mock niceties were almost as hard to bear as taking Red's beatings. He wasn't making love to her, no matter how his words sounded, and inwardly, she despised the two men equally.

Eddie used his arms to lift her up and down upon him, as he breathed on her back and neck. He ran his hands across her sticky flesh to massage her exposed belly and breasts, moaning loudly. Tori swallowed hard, her head tilted back against him so that her neck pulled taught in the front.

Reaching up, his fingers slid lightly across her windpipe, feeling the bands of cartilage underneath. In this position, he could have crushed it and killed her easily, and it was nights like this she prayed that he would, and end her suffering and the sorrow that she never allowed to show.

When he finally finished, he pushed her off of him, and then stood, giving Red a satiated grin. The rest of the guys had found spots to curl up or stretch out for the night, and she would finally be left alone. She lay in a heap on the floor, drifting in and out of consciousness, her mind numb and unable to think clearly in her exhaustion as she listened to the storm finally blowing itself out.

After a few hours, she found herself awake, and stumbled through the building naked, until she found a bathroom. The water in the sink only ran cold, but she used it to wash away the blood and what they had left inside her. She made her way back to the room with the couch and located her cleanish garments, just as she had left them. She put on the lace bra and panties, and then pulled the shirt over her head, her arms aching with the motion.

Her pants were tight against her sore posterior, and she moved gingerly, carrying her boots as she went out and found a large room with a stage at the front and rows of long benches below. Pushing her right shoulder into a corner, she leaned her head against the wall and studied the strange place. She had never been inside a church before, and wondered what went on inside such an oddly decorated room. Breathing deeply, she eventually drifted off to sleep.

Forgiveness

Today will be different, she told herself with a deep breath. Climbing out of the car, Tori steeled herself for what lay before her. Watching the others who were entering the building, she noticed the wide variety in the way they were dressed.

There were some who were as plainly dressed as herself, but the styles went all the way up to men in suits and ladies in brightly colored flowing dresses. Tori could not resist the feeling of being on the outside, seeing their excitement. The air seemed electrified by their enthusiasm and obvious joy, but it did not extend to her.

Terry led her inside, and they took a seat towards the back, at the end of one of the long pews, next to the aisle in the center. A few of the men came by to shake his hand in welcome, and he introduced her simply by saying, "This is my friend, Tori," which was met with a variety of silent responses.

Taking their seats, she suddenly realized these people may think the two of them were a couple, unless he brought lost vagabonds with him regularly. If that were the case, she would only be the latest misplaced soul.

Her memory fresh as to her last and only visit to a church, Tori sat watching, taking everything in. She noticed the piano and organ at the front and the booming sounds that they made. The crowd opened books full of music, called hymnals, and sang loudly, sometimes standing to do so.

The pastor made announcements about youth activities, visitation, men's meetings, and choir practice. They sang again, and a set of shiny flat bowls was passed around so that people could put money into them. Afterwards, everyone sat quietly while the pastor stood up to speak.

Tori began to feel out of place in the crowded room, as if she were still naked, stumbling around in the dark. The man at the front opened a very large volume and placed it on the podium. She half expected him to start with, *My name is . . .,* the thought bringing a slight smile to her lips. Instead, his first words were, "Today, I want to talk about forgiveness."

Immediately, Tori's heart began to pound. He went on to say that there were different types of forgiveness, explaining some of them in detail, such as the forgiveness of God. She listened intently, her hands folded in her lap in front of her as she pressed her palms together tightly.

"The forgiveness of God is great!" he bellowed. "But to have and accept it, we must also have forgiveness in our hearts. We must forgive those who have wronged us."

Tori could feel her pulse hammering in her ears. *He wants me to forgive people? The Dragons, for the things they did to me?* Her jaw dropped in an incredulous expression before she clamped it shut.

Terry reached over and slid his hand between hers. Looping her fingers with his, he gave her a light squeeze.

Looking over at him, she saw he watched the front, a slight smile on his face. His thumb rubbed gently against the side of her hand in a comforting manner, and Tori did not pull it away, choosing to allow him to touch her for the time being.

The speaker continued, "Forgiving our fellow man is easy, compared to forgiving ourselves."

Tori felt the stab of pain in her heart, like this stranger could see inside her and knew what she was thinking.

"But I tell you," he went on in a softer tone, "You must forgive your own sins if you are ever to turn away from them and walk in a new life."

She stiffened in her seat, *a new life? Oh, my God, he's talking to me.* Tori glanced around anxiously, but everyone watched the preacher attentively, paying no attention to her or the man who squeezed her hand.

The sermon ended, and the music played again, a slow sad song. The crowd stood with their heads bowed as they softly sang or hummed. Tori could feel Terry's palm burning as it pressed against hers, but she did not want to let it go. She clung to him, the tears heavy inside her, as she wanted to find the reconciliation the pastor had spoken of, only not sure if she could or would ever find the forgiveness inside her heart.

Terry stroked her with his thumb, the two of them leaning slightly against one another. Tall enough to see the top of her downturned head, he wanted desperately for her to find the peace she deserved.

Soon, the song ended, and with a quick squeeze and a smile, he released her. Everyone began to exit the building to go about their busy lives. Preparing to leave, Tori could feel her breathing drop to short spasms as Terry led her towards the front of the building instead of allowing her to escape out the back.

She wanted to make a dash for his car as he held her elbow, guiding her closer to the man who had spoken to her so sternly. Shaking the pastor's hand, he introduced her again, "Brother Thomas, this is Tori, the young lady I've been telling you about."

I knew it—he was talking to me!

Brother Thomas smiled broadly, with straight white teeth, as he offered her his hand. Tori did not move to take it, and he folded his fingers back at his side without comment.

143

The two men spoke briefly, then the man in the suit handed her a book she had never owned: a bible. With a final smile before he walked away, he told her it was a gift from the church, and that he hoped it would guide her to find tranquility in her life. She stared down at the plain black cover for a moment, and then folded her arms around it, pressing it against her breasts. Quietly, she followed Terry to his car so they could leave the emptying parking lot.

Arriving back at the house at shortly after noon, lunch was being prepared. Tori held the text against her chest and moved swiftly up to her room. She had accepted the gift, but climbing the stairs with it, she wasn't sure she would ever read it.

Her heart pounded as she slid the book into the top drawer of the dresser, next to her journal. Looking at the notebook for a moment, she pulled it out, along with the pencil. She had only made a few entries, but this was something she felt the need to record.

Placing the date at the top of a new page, she wrote about her first experience at a place of worship. She included details about the sermon that she wanted to think about later and work out for herself. When she finished, she returned the notebook and pencil to the drawer and headed back down stairs, humming lightly as she went.

After a small meal, Tori spent the rest of the day working on the '62 Honda Dream that had sat in the garage gathering dust all those years. She had pulled the engine out and worked slowly at rebuilding it.

Brandon had located as many tools for her as he could, using the opportunity to clean out the garage as he searched, and he threw away things that were broken or old beyond use. He toyed with the idea of setting up a workbench to organize everything on in the back.

Gazing down at her grease coated fingers, Tori

remembered the first lesson Eddie had given her about motorcycles, before they had left the bush camp. He had found her lack of knowledge frustrating, and pushed her every day after that to learn about the thing he cherished most: his bike. She had learned quickly, and that seemed to appease him to a small extent. His '79 Electra Glide was a beautiful machine, all black and chrome, and she wondered what had become of the motorcycles that were left standing outside the farmhouse when she had finished with their owners.

Late in the afternoon, Tori felt surprised to see Max walking up the long driveway. Setting her work down, she used a red rag to wipe at her hands as she ambled out to meet him. He smiled as his eyes swept over the scene, taking in the sight of the gutted frame and small parts.

"You know," he began, "My dad was into motorcycles when I was a kid, so I learned a bit about them, but it's been a while since I've been around any. Mind if I watch?" he asked, swooshing his long bangs out of his eyes.

Tori smiled at the movement, having always had a certain fondness for him ever since the day they met, and she first held his hand on the way to the café. "Not at all," she replied warmly not minding the interruption.

Reclaiming the screwdriver she had been using to tighten a few bolts, she felt glad things were working out and that he had come around for a visit. They spent the rest of the evening looking at parts and chatting about bikes, the store, and the old days. Cleaning up and putting things away, Tori could feel him watching her.

Out of the blue, he asked, "You ever think about your parents?"

A little stunned by the question, she reminded him, "I don't know who my parents are, Max," without even looking up.

"That's not what I mean," he stated, somewhat irritated. "I know you don't know them, but do you ever think about them. Who they might be? What they might be like? Are they looking for you?" Tori continued to straighten the tools without answering him, so he waited patiently, knowing this to be her way.

When she had the items arranged to her satisfaction, she met his gaze and answered, "Sometimes. I think about them living in a house like this one, with other people around, like grandparents and aunts and uncles." She almost appeared wistful as she continued, "And I do wonder if they are looking for me. Part of me is hoping that someday I might have the chance to find out, but deep down I know that it would not be a good thing if it were to ever happen." Max gave her a confused look but said nothing.

"You see," Tori went on slowly, sharing more of her story than he had heard with the others, "Even though the group of men who raised me are dead, there are others who are equally as terrifying who would hurt people I care about, or who care about me, if it would help them get what they want. That's why I can't stay here," her tone grew sad as she finished. "I'm going to stay until I'm emancipated, but after that I'm going to go someplace quiet, where I won't be risking the lives and well-being of those around me."

Tori knew she was well into her twenties, but the Feds made the rules, and she would have to play by them. If that were not the case, she would already be gone. As it were, she would bide her time until they gave her enough leeway she could get away from their schemes, but she didn't bother to explain any further; *he doesn't need to know all that*, she rationalized.

Max considered her words, quietly nodding his head. He thought about the night he and his friends had foolishly gone out partying at the little bar down from their apartment. He had been fairly wasted by the time it ended, but he had seen what she had done to those men with a simple stick. If there were people like her out there lurking around or looking for her, he understood why she felt the need to hide someplace quiet. He could tell he had hit a raw nerve with his new friend, and that she spent a great deal more time thinking about these things than she let on.

Moving up onto the porch, the pair sat on the large swing and rocked gently back and forth as the darkness fell. He tried to get more out of her about her plans, where she might be headed or what she wanted to do, but she skillfully avoided revealing what she had in mind. Deep down, Tori knew when she left, it would be sudden, and she would never return. But for the time being, this was her home, and these were her friends, and she liked that. She intended to enjoy it for as long as she could, and prayed it would not have a great price in the end.

Loose Ends

In the weeks and months that followed, Tori had minor setbacks, but her friends were there to help her through and encourage her that she could make it. By the time she started her fifth month, almost everyone who had been in the halfway house when she came in had moved on. She had hugged each one of them at their departure and told them to keep in touch, but secretly in her heart, she knew the time loomed ever closer that she would disappear, and no one would be able to reach her.

Lins was the last to leave, and she took her parting the hardest of all. Tori had never had a female friend like Lins. They were about the same age, and their lives were much more alike than she had thought possible when she came to LA. During their time together, they had laughed, cried, shopped, gotten manicures, and shared stories. Tori had no family to speak of, but if she ever thought of someone like a sister, Lindsey was it; this had been the first time she truly saw the world with the eyes of a woman.

Of course, those who remained all knew how hard losing another person would be on the girl. She had lost everyone she had ever been close to. They all hoped she would be strong enough to make it through, but each secretly feared it would push her over the edge, and she would fall back into her old ways. For one full week after Lins moved out, Tori was not left alone once she left the house. Someone either gave her a ride to work, or met her at the house to walk with

148

her. In the evenings, someone made sure she made it home, all the way up to the door.

The last night of that week, everyone met at the house for dinner. Gathered around the table again, Tori felt odd. Many of the people who were there the first time had been replaced, and she did not get to know any of the new people who came into the house, purposely keeping her distance.

She was content with the friends that were left, not wanting to add to her own or anyone else's pain when her own time came to go. During dinner, Tori thanked everyone for being so supportive of her, and asked only half kidding, "Now, stop hovering over me. I'm a big girl and I can take care of myself." Everyone laughed, but no one felt nearly as certain.

That night, when Tori went to her room, she wrote in her journal about her experiences and how she missed the people who had gone. Writing a small passage about each one, she felt at peace, and slept better that night than she had in a while.

The next morning, during their work out, she told Terry about feeling better and how she wished they really would give her some room. He must have been listening or believed, because they allowed her to walk to work that day alone; that day and every day afterwards.

The week after Lindsey left the house, Tori attended her last AA meeting. The meetings had always been hard for her, even after she could admit she had a drinking problem. She spoke to people when she had to, but she never reached out to any of them, preferring to socialize with the boys at the shop or those at the house.

On the last night, she almost felt like it was her graduation, knowing she would not be coming back. Not once had she stood up and said those famous words, "My name is . . ." and as she left for the last time, she wondered for a brief moment if she should have, but only for a moment. Tori was tying up the loose ends of LA, and making plans for what would be next, and she felt glad to put this particular part behind her.

Things were pretty hectic at the shop the next week. In two weeks, the large *Indelible* promotion that Terry had been putting together would be taking place. There were plans to have them play at the store in a private concert, have an autograph session, and a contest for someone from the area to win the chance to play on stage with them during the first concert on their next tour.

A radio station and a few other businesses were involved, and things were running smoothly. However, Terry relied on Tori immensely to take charge of the store and of all of the paperwork, including making the deposits and directing the employees.

Tori made her way up to the shop even earlier since she essentially ran the place. She had really settled into the position, and wanted to make sure she still had time to play in the mornings before everyone arrived.

She had been making her plans, the secret ones that no one knew about, in preparation for her emancipation that would take place a few days before the private concert, where the winner of the contest would be named. She had wanted to leave the same day as the meeting, but realizing that Terry needed her, she knew she would stay until after the promo ended; she owed him that.

One such morning, three days before the committee meeting, Tori felt like things might unravel. She had gone in at 7:30 to count the tills and prepare the deposit, as usual. Once everything had been locked in the safe, she made her way out to the front and opened the instrument case. Removing her key from the lock, she hummed a song by the group who would be taking over her store; *it's not long, and*

I'll leave this place behind.

Plugging in the leads and adjusting the controls, she decided, *I think I'll have some fun with a couple of their songs. He's not the only one who can play them;* her thoughts were filled with disdain. Brian Madson had been in the week before to pick up the custom that Terry had built for him, and they had gotten to meet for the first time.

Immediately, she felt on the defensive, as the man turned out to be a real jerk. *Of course he is,* she rationalized to herself in retrospect, *he's rich and famous and better than everyone else, especially you.* Where most girls fell all over themselves for the chance to be close to men like Brian, Tori wanted nothing of him, and the experience made her long to be finished and gone from that place.

Running her fingers slowly along the fret board, she went through one of the band's songs, feeling the cords out before she brought them up to speed. A few minutes later, her fingers danced across the strings, and she began to get that sensation.

The guitar had become a drug for her, one that made her euphoric, where she could get lost in the feeling and forget about the things that loomed about her, threatening her life, future, and those she cared about. Letting herself live in the moment, she could feel the rest of the world melt away, free to let her music express what lay in the depths of her soul.

Tori stood on the little stage as she played, but she had no plans to ever do so publicly or even for another person. Her gift was something she did for herself, by herself, and she liked it that way. Becoming engrossed in the sounds she created, she began to sway her body in time, and her hair fell down over her face, obstructing her view.

She closed her eyes, allowing her spirit to become a part of the riffs as they flowed out of her. Finishing the melody, she lifted her head, her hair hanging down in front of her face. Reaching to her forehead, she ran her fingers along her scalp from the front to the back, and then through the long strands to pull it out of her face, a smile of ecstasy on her lips.

Tori opened her eyes, startled to discover she wasn't alone. Terry had come in early to meet with Brian Madson and Collin Graham, who liked to be involved in the planning at the ground level for events such as this one.

They had entered while she played, lost in her addiction, and had stood silently watching her movement as she tossed her ebony tresses behind her. Slightly embarrassed, and angry at being caught, more or less, she unstrapped the guitar, intending to put it away and get on with her day.

Collin had other plans, stepping up to her while grinning from ear to ear. "Hey, that's pretty good," he complimented her as he introduced himself to the dark haired beauty, "I'm Collin... Graham. Bass player." Tori accepted his outstretched palm in her discombobulated state, and he held it firmly, rubbing the back with his thumb as they conversed.

"So, listen, would you like to jam for a bit? I'd love to play with you." He used the pun out of habit, wondering if she would bite. Giving her his best grin as he cajoled her, he mentally lamented, *Brian said she was a bitch; he neglected to mention how gorgeous!*

Tori shook her dark waves, giving him an awkward smile, "I need to get the store ready to open." She looked down at her hand, still entrapped in his. *Damn it. If I pull it away, then I look anti-social, and I've been working so hard on that.* His fingers produced an odd sensation in the pit of her stomach, and she felt conflicted by the tingle in her skin as he caressed it.

"Well, like I said, you're really good. Some other time then?" he turned on the charm, flashing eyes and teeth.

Continuing to keep him at bay, she shyly admitted with a

small giggle, "No one was supposed to hear that. I play for myself, not for other people." Her wider smile hinted that she enjoyed the attention he gave her, their physical contact more moving than their slow conversation.

Brian chose that instant to interrupt them, walking up to announce quite loudly, "Hey, knock it off you two. We all have work to do," and he practically dragged Collin away from her. He would never admit she was any good, thinking to himself, that imitation might be the sincerest form of flattery, but he would rather not have her butchering his music, changing it the way she had been when the small group walked in. He had not liked the girl since he met her, finding her to be standoffish and conniving, and his opinion wasn't about to change anytime soon, even if his best friend did want to fuck her.

The three men went on about their business, standing next to the far glass counter while they discussed how things should be set up for the upcoming events. While she hung the guitar back in the case, Tori could feel Collin watching her, and stole a glance in their direction as she locked it up.

He flashed a grin at her when he saw her peek, and she could feel the color rise to her cheeks at having been caught by him for the second time in one day. She went about the work of opening the registers and inspecting the store, but everywhere she went, she could feel his gaze upon her.

Tori let Max and Derrick in at 10:00 am and set them to work on the list of chores Terry had given her. They had worked out where things were going to be located for the autograph session, which would be the first event in the series taking place at their location. They were expecting to have lots of customers in the store, so all of the shelves and racks would need to be stuffed for the extra sales.

While Tori was in the back getting the deposit, Collin reappeared, trapping her in the door frame of the office with his tanned arms. She shifted her gaze nervously as he made his case, "So, how about dinner then? Surely you like to eat." *Man, this girl is smokin'*, his eyes stared at her perfect pink lips as he waited for her reply.

She caught a whiff of his aftershave, liking the scent more than she cared to admit. Smiling politely, she reached up to lay her hand on his chest, "That sounds really exciting, but I do have work to do. And I have plans later, thanks." Pushing him back away from her, she closed the office and went on her way.

He watched her as she walked, liking the way her rear end swayed below the ends of her long dark hair. Collin wasn't used to being turned down by girls. Since the band had their first hit five years prior, things had come pretty easy for him. *Oh yeah, this one'll be a challenge, and I like challenges.* She might not fall right into bed with him, but he discerned he could get her if he played his cards right. Rubbing the burning spot on his chest where she had touched him, he chuckled, *it's just a matter of time.*

Tori walked the two blocks to the bank, her head spinning. *What in the hell could a man like Collin Graham want with me, besides a quick romp?* She didn't like the way he made her palms sweaty or her heart beat like a thoroughbred on race day.

Besides, she had completely sworn off men since Enrique left, and in her heart, she still loved him. She didn't think about him so much anymore, but she wasn't ready to admit he was gone for good. Trudging along, thoughts about her lost loves swirled inside her head, darkening her mood.

By the time she made it back to the store, Tori was almost in a fit of rage, angry at the world that gave her people to love, only to take them away. She felt that life somehow plotted against her, and she had no intention of adding Collin to her list. Pulling the glass door open to go back inside, she made a solemn oath she would not allow that to happen.

Making her way through to check on the progress with preparations, Tori noted that Terry and the other two men were gone. She breathed a sigh of relief, hoping she could avoid any further contact with the man who pursued her. Eyeing the white guitar as it hung in the rack, she felt a pang of sadness knowing she would not be able to take it with her when she left; *another love I will lose*, she thought with a sigh.

The next day, the autograph session took place without a hitch. Tori managed to avoid the band entirely and busied herself with running the store. Terry had been right; the place teemed with customers, and in no time the fifty slots for the contest were filled.

Tori had felt Collin watching her, but when she looked his way, he would turn, suddenly interested in something else close at hand. She noted the way he played the girls, confident her decision to avoid him had been sound. *And in a few days, I can kiss this place, and jackasses like those two, goodbye.*

Destiny or Fate

The committee meeting rapidly approached, being only two days away. Tori reminded Terry she would need the day off, but promised to come by and let him know how things had gone. The morning of the meeting, she awoke with an uneasy lump in the pit of her stomach. Slipping into her workout clothes, she made her way downstairs and out of the door as usual. She pushed herself extra hard that morning, hoping to drain some of the nervous energy she felt trapped inside her.

Making it back to the house, she found Sharon already in the kitchen, as if she were waiting for her. Tori made a point to stop and speak to the older woman, as she respected her and appreciated all she had done to help her on her path. Grabbing her bottle of water and an orange, she sat at the table so the pair could talk.

"Are you nervous?" Sharon inquired with a smile.

Tori admitted, "A bit anxious, I guess." They talked quietly about the proceedings and who would be attending. Tori felt fairly certain Eli would not be there. She had never really spoken of him to anyone, and so their night together remained a secret as far as she knew. However, his having been reassigned was suspicious, to say the least.

Tori assumed Jim Godfry would be attending, and perhaps Warren La Buff. She hoped Debra would make it, but wasn't getting her hopes up. Beyond that, she had no idea who to expect.

Sharon assured her that she and Brandon would be there and that Terry had given a statement that would be read. Tori knew a lot of the proceedings rested on formality, but there was always the possibility they could make her wait longer or flat deny her release, and the thought of that scared her.

The clock staring down at her read almost 7:00 when Tori finally stood, announcing she should get ready. Making her way into the shower, she pushed the thoughts of what lay ahead out of her mind. She needed to focus on this day, as nothing would follow if it were not successful. After the meeting, she could finalize her plans for the future.

Tori put on her bra and panties and covered her scar. She had been thinking about the tattoo to cover it, but still had not been able to settle on a design. She chose to wear a white shirt, along with her customary jeans and boots. Brushing out her ebony locks, she approved of the glossy sheen. With everything perfect, she made her way back downstairs, where Brandon and Sharon were waiting.

The three of them drove to the courthouse, and they would be meeting with the committee in a closed session. Entering the small chamber, Tori noted that Doug Seeming had come with the group, along with Dr. Bennet.

She had not forgiven him for doing this to her, as his expert opinion had put her in that situation. She hoped he felt stupid, as she had not grown at all since coming into custody, and it should be obvious at this point that he was wrong.

Of course La Buff and Godfry were both there, as Tori had predicted, so the only two main members who were missing were Debra and Eli. Although curious where they had gone to, she did not dare ask on such a precarious occasion.

The final man in the room a stranger to her, she sat staring at his lined face. An older man, with almost no hair, the few that remained were a silvery grey that matched his skin. The man pursed his lips at her and did not smile. His look made her knotted stomach flop as she folded her hands in her lap.

Special Agent James Godfry called the meeting to order, although no one was actually speaking when he did so. In the interest of formality, he read a brief statement as to Tori's case, outlining their agreement and her fulfillment of those terms.

He also gave Dr. Bennet a chance to speak as to his medical opinion of her, and he again described how he had determined her age. Although she did not realize it, she gave him an icy stare as he spoke, the anger simmering just below the surface. When he finished, Doug Seeming reported their progress towards finding her identity.

"I hate to admit it," he stated with obvious disappointment, "But we have been unsuccessful at finding any leads as to Tori's origins."

She felt a mixture of sadness and relief at the news, and maintained her placid composure.

"We went back as far as twenty years with missing children files," he continued with a sigh, "We did blood testing on known relatives of those missing; everything we could think of. We got nothing. I believe it's safe to say, well I hate to use the word safe, but we can be pretty strong in saying, her true identity will never be located."

Tori stared at her lap as he finished speaking, trying to hide the sense of relief she felt. *Thank God... my family will never be placed in danger because of me.*

After everyone from Chicago had given their part, Sharon read Terry's letter aloud. Brief but genuine, Tori felt glad she had decided to stay through another few days to help him. His words were kind and convincing, describing how she had grown as an employee, always been respectful and hardworking, and capable of handling responsibility. He finished by saying he knew she would someday move on to other things, and she would be greatly missed. Tears stung her eyes as she tried to blink them back, knowing that day was not so far away.

The Tates each had a turn to speak about what they had witnessed, and Sharon spoke of her relationship with Lins and how she had watched the girl blossom into a confident young woman. Tori began to feel as if they were trying to make her cry, and she caught a tear at the corner of her eye, dabbing it with the tip of her finger.

Brandon at least had the kindness to be less emotional, talking about what he had observed with her relationships and how she had poured herself into rebuilding the motorcycle that stood in his garage, shining like new. Now that it was running, he confided that he wished he could get ahold of the actual owner, who had left it behind, to return it.

At last, the older man identified himself, "Tori, my name is Judge William Carlton, and I'm going to give the final ruling on your case. Before I make that decision, I would like to hear from you. What are your ideas for the future and where do you see yourself going from here?"

She drew in a deep breath, knowing she could not simply blurt out all the plans she had been making, as this was a time for finesse and intrepidity. Exhaling the breath slowly, she could feel herself slipping into the role, and she began by admitting she had a dark history.

She passed quickly over her transgressions that had been laid out before the committee in Chicago, and her brief infidelity that had occurred with Enrique and what became of that. She ended by speaking about her efforts to improve herself, her church adventure, her journal and its aide in finding a clear path, and the AA meetings that she attended every week. She relayed briefly her joy at the friendships she had formed and embellished as she saw fit, and in a way felt as if she were trying to sell the man a new shiny guitar.

In the end, she hoped that she had polished the story enough and that she had conveyed sincerity as she explained that she wanted to settle down and build a life for herself there, where she had begun to put down roots. She could see the smile on Sharon's face as she spoke, and it gave her confidence that this was a pleasing path to embrace, one that would help her case.

Sticking to safer tactics, she made no mention of her fear of what was coming, or the fact that she knew she was a pawn that the FBI intended to play with as they willed. She also did not mention her relief that her family had not and would not ever be located and that her identity was locked away somewhere in a hidden vault not even she could open.

Upon hearing her words, the judge asked her to step outside so that they could discuss her case and come to a decision. Rising slowly, she gave them a small smile, her intestines still twisting in knots. She passed through the door, closing it behind her.

Making her way down the hall, she found a small waiting area and purchased a bottle of water out of the vending machine. They were several stories up, so she stood next to the large window that surveyed the wide expanse of LA while gulping it anxiously.

It seemed like hours, but in fact only a few minutes had passed before Sharon came and asked her to return to the tiny room. Walking in, Tori studied the faces to see if she could ascertain the verdict. Most were smiling, and she could feel the relief wash over her, as surely that meant good news.

Again, Judge Carlton spoke. "Tori, I want to congratulate you on the steps you have taken. You have come a long way in a short time, and that is commendable. I also want you to know, I've made a note as to your disagreement to the necessity of being emancipated. However, as the expert, Dr.

Bennet's evaluation will stand."

Setting her jaw, she tried to hold the anger out of her eyes at the decision.

Tapping a folder before him, the older man continued, "That means that you will be bound by this judgment, and your established age will be sixteen years as of today. Furthermore, you will be emancipated according to the laws of the State of California, and you will not be permitted to drink or vote until you reach the proper age according to the date of birth that has been established for you. Do you have any questions about these guidelines as I have described them?"

Tori managed to force a small smile as she shook her head emphatically.

He continued, his voice confident in his role, "If you have no questions, then it is my pleasure to pronounce you emancipated by the power of this court. May you have a long and happy life."

Everyone in the room breathed a sigh of relief and Sharon leapt to her feet to hug her. She gushed on about how excited they were that she had decided to stay in LA and that they would be more than willing to help her look for a place of her own.

Tori felt glad she had not told them her real plans. Walking out of the building, she thought about what it really meant, and she could not help wondering if being freed was her destiny or her fate.

Remaining after the room had cleared, Dr. Bennet, Warren La Buff, and James Godfry sat in the tiny chamber. Leaning back in his chair, La Buff lamented, "I think we should have brought the judge in on this. He isn't going to be too pleased when he finds out he was duped."

"How's he going to find out?" Dr. Bennet countered. "The only way anyone will ever know is if her identity is discovered and a birth certificate is produced, which it won't be. Otherwise, no one will question my judgment."

La Buff narrowed his eyes at the doctor's words. "Don't get cocky. You better hope no one finds out. I cannot believe I'm even involved in this."

Godfry gave him a wry grin, "Like you've never done anything that was off the books. Come on, this is perfect. The judge signed the papers." He turned his palms toward the ceiling, indicating his hands were clean. "The girl practically works for us already. All we do now is give her some time on her own, and then we reel her in. You guys can get her off on her little assignment, and when she's done with that, we offer her a full time job doing what she's best at."

The three men stared at one another, considering what Tori Farrell was best at, the pause in the conversation growing long. La Buff nodded slowly, "All I can say is, you're fucking with a girl who has murdered about a dozen of the worst men we have ever had on the books. You better *hope* she never finds out you did this to her on purpose, under false pretenses. I don't think she would bat an eyelash at taking care of any of *us* in the same manner."

Like New

The trio chatted non-stop as they made their way back to the halfway house. Sharon appeared the most excited, Tori observed, but Brandon looked pretty pleased himself. She smiled genuinely at the couple, content with their happiness for her.

She had been given a card to carry that stated she had been emancipated, so she would be able to conduct business as an adult, but she could also get a copy of the full file if she ever needed one. She had placed the card in her wallet and kept peeking at it as they drove, as if she were afraid it would disappear. She could get a regular picture ID as well, whenever she got herself settled, and mentally added it to her list of tasks for the future.

The group stopped for a late lunch at a large restaurant, and Tori could feel the pulse of the crowd that scurried about them while they ate. Sharon asked her questions and made suggestions, and she allowed the woman her plans for a place near the house so they could remain close.

Brandon sat in silence, watching the girl's expression as the meal went on, and his wife spoke. He had heard her say she planned to build her life near them, but her body language made him wonder if she had something to hide. He fondly recalled the first time he laid eyes on the tall young woman, when she had exited the tunnel at LAX, *so much about her has changed; and yet so much is the same.*

After their meal, the three climbed back into his grey

Toyota, and they rode in a more peaceful quiet the rest of the way. As soon as the car stopped in the drive, Tori leapt out and announced she needed to visit the shop. She knew the guys there would be on pins and needles, wanting to know the outcome.

She made it to the glass door in record time, practically bouncing over the counter. Opening her wallet, she showed Terry the card, and he gave a loud shout. A little freer with the hugs that day than she had ever been, even Derrick got one. They were still standing around, laughing and talking, when all four members of *Indelible* walked through the door.

Brian immediately inquired what the celebration was about, and before she could head him off, Max had blurted out, "Tori got emancipated this afternoon."

She tried to hide her displeasure, having wanted to keep the news to the confines of her small group of friends. She drew a deep breath to clear her thoughts and not spoil the mood. Changing the topic, she introduced herself to the drummer and lead singer of the group, Chuck Stotts and Cody Pierce, respectively. Making the effort, she shook each man's hand in the process. *This is a day for celebrating, after all*, and she managed a small smile to boot.

After hearing the news, Collin had gotten a funny look on his face. Working his way next to her, he leaned in close enough to whisper in her ear, "So… you're not eighteen?"

Tori blinked at him calmly, thinking about the paper in her wallet for a moment. *Hmm, he still smells good*, she noted. She had not intended to tell him anything about herself, but now that she had her freedom, what would it hurt? "It's a really long story," she replied, giving him a coy grin.

"I don't have a date for dinner. We should go, and you can tell me all about it," the bass player countered her with a teasing tug on a few locks of her hair.

Tori thought it would be better to refuse, but something in the angry glare Brian gave her made her change her mind. "You wanna pick me up or meet somewhere?" she cooed sweetly.

"No time like the present," he offered her his arm. Taking it, she allowed him to whisk her away, pleased at the sour look that remained on Brian's features.

Outside, they climbed into the limo. She looked around the car in amazement, and he smiled at her awed expression. Knowing he watched her, she could feel her palms begin to sweat, and she felt unsure that she had made a wise choice.

"What do you like to eat?" he probed, his voice deep and rich.

Tori's heart began to thump, but she managed to reply, "I'm a meat and veggies kind of girl."

He grinned at her riposte and instructed the driver to head back to the hotel. She shot him a questioning gaze at their destination, but he only continued to smile in response.

The hotel turned out to be spectacular. The foyer had a high ceiling, filled with glass and light. Tori thought he would take her to the restaurant, but instead he led her to his room, which she noted to be equally stunning. As soon as they were inside, he pulled out a menu, and they picked out steaks, salads and vegetables. *I wonder if he always eats like this, or if it's only because I'm here,* she pondered while chewing her cheek and studying his profile.

Walking around the suite, she felt reminded how far removed her life had become from what it had once been. Dropping her jacket on an expensive looking chair, she stopped in front of the large wall of glass that looked out over the city. Admiring the view, she exhaled loudly as the sun set, and lights began to twinkle across the skyline.

Collin sidled up beside her, focusing on her bare arms for the first time, "Would you like something to drink? Beer, wine?"

Tori waved her hand, "Naw, I can't drink that stuff."

Taking a step back, he asked in a scoffing sort of tone, "Who's gonna know? I'm not gonna tell anyone." He smiled again, still trying to play it smooth, and keep his eye on the prize.

Turning to face him squarely, Tori realized she stood at the point where she would have to choose. She had a chance to stay clean, but the temptation would always be there. In a stiff voice, she replied, "That's not what I mean. I mean *I won't.*" She laid her right hand flat against the upper part of her chest for emphasis.

Staring at her for a moment, he got an odd, almost angry, look on his face, but said nothing else.

"I would like water though, if you don't mind." She smiled, but suspected he regretted bringing her there.

Turning his back, he walked away, leaving her alone for several minutes. When he returned, he held a bottle of water for her in one hand, and a glass bottle in the other.

Tori took the frosty beverage, her face expressionless as she felt unwelcome after his long absence.

He motioned out the window, waving his second beer at the sun as it sank into the shadows. "Beautiful here," he made another attempt at small talk.

She sipped her water, not bothering to reply.

He cut his eyes over at her, and then chugged his beverage. Their mood broken, neither of them felt comfortable. A loud knock at the door interrupted the tense moment, and a waiter pushed their dinner into the room. The awkward silence continued as they sat down to eat the delicious meal. If the company had been only half as good, it would have been a wonderful experience.

Chewing slowly, Tori thought about the men she had been with throughout her life. If this would be considered a date, she had not been on many. She sighed deeply, thinking how the only thing she really had going for her was her body, and that, she did not want to use. Staring down at her plate, she suspected he hadn't really asked her there to hear her story.

This man probably couldn't care less about me personally. He only wanted one thing, the same thing most men want: another conquest. She suddenly felt overly warm, her anger beginning to grow. *I gotta get out of here.* Standing, she spit her words curtly, "Thanks for the lovely evening," and grabbing her jacket, headed for the door.

He watched her go, still eating and drinking from his third bottle. *She wasn't all that after she got her jacket off anyways; some serious scars for damn sure,* he muttered to himself in consolation.

Tori made it down to the lobby, where she asked the clerk to call her a cab. A few minutes later, she sat in the back seat, headed for home. The ride seemed a lot longer from inside the taxi than it had from the window of the limo. While she rode, her thoughts churned. *Taking care of the physical needs of some spoiled man isn't part of my job; at least not anymore.*

She swore to herself she would choose the next man she lay with far more carefully than she had in the past. Of course, she hadn't taken the alcohol either, and that probably helped her keep her resolve. She wasn't happy with the outcome, but then again she felt pretty confident she would still feel the same if she had given in to him, only to be discarded afterwards.

By the time she arrived at the house, she had the words to a song rolling around in her head. Stomping up the stairs, she grabbed her journal and put them down on paper. Thinking she liked the way they sounded, she decided she would make sure she had time in the morning to play and try for some music to go with her lyrics. It may have been her first attempt at song writing, but from the peace it gave her in her chest, she had a feeling it would not be her last.

Sitting in the wooden rocker, she thought about the plans she had made. She knew where she had to go first when she left, but after that, only an idea of what she wanted. She had learned so many skills at the shop; she felt confident she could run a small business if she were able to open one.

She had enjoyed rebuilding the bike, too. Rocking slowly, she allowed herself to imagine rebuilding them for a living, buying broken down motorcycles and making them like new again. In a way, that's what Brandon, Sharon and the others had done for her; taken someone who had been broken and made her like new. But soon, it would be solely up to her to stay that way.

His Little Girl

When Tori awoke the next morning, she could feel her heart pounding with anticipation. She rushed to get to the store as early as she could, hoping she would not be interrupted. Scurrying about, she finished up the paperwork and opened the registers. Finally, she made a quick trip around the store, and then headed for the instruments on the wall. Pulling down her favorite, her fingers trembled with excitement.

Setting up quickly, she began to run through the music she had mentally written the night before. After a few minutes, she pulled out the piece of paper, the edge jagged where she had removed it from the spiral. Laying it on top of the amp, she played the guitar and went through the words together, and then she began to sing.

Tori didn't know how to write music on paper, so she made some notes for herself on the page of lyrics as to what she had in mind. She continued to play through and sing, making changes until she had it exactly the way she wanted. Folding up the paper to put back in her pocket, she put the guitar away, ready to open the doors when the time came. All day, her mind kept returning to the song, like an obsession she couldn't shake.

The next morning went much the same, with Tori taking out the guitar to work on her creation. This time, however, she knew what she wanted, and she practiced it many times, until it sounded the way she heard it in her mind, and she could sing it the way she had envisioned.

Now, all she had to do was wait, and hope for the opportunity to play the song for Collin Graham. Not because she ever wanted to be famous or anything like that, but rather because she had written the song for him. It held her story and explained her as a person. Basically, all the things he had ignored about her the night she had dinner with him at his hotel. She didn't have a lot of time though, as the contest would be the next day, with the finals the following afternoon.

That evening, Terry came in, and everyone worked to set up for the contest. Those who were going to play in the competition had already registered during the autograph session. At five minutes each, it would take over four hours to hear them all.

The store had a very large sales floor, so the fixtures were shifted to create a larger seating area around the small stage and chairs were set up and roped off. A judge's table had been placed along the wall end of the instrument case where a group of execs from the record label would sit to choose the winners.

While she worked, Tori thought about her plans for after the event ended, and she would be on her way. She wondered if she shouldn't mention to her boss that she intended to leave. She had not planned to do so. In fact, she had not planned on telling anyone; she would simply get up the next day and be gone. Thinking about it at the moment made her fidget anxiously.

Finally, she made her decision. Staying late, Tori waited until everyone had departed, and she had him to herself.

Terry beamed, finally beginning to feel they were ready for their big event. He stood next to the stage area, admiring their work as she waited patiently for her chance to clear the air. He smiled at her excitedly, eager to see how this would work out for him.

She liked seeing him so happy, and for a moment thought about reconsidering her choice. He grinned broadly when he thanked her for staying after to make sure everything would be perfect.

For a moment, she allowed him to gush on; then holding up her hand, she announced, "That's not really the reason why I'm here."

Terry's smile shrank a bit, "What're you talking about?"

"I have something I need to discuss with you," she answered quietly.

Sensing her heightened emotions, he reached out to squeeze her upper arm, "Then spit it out. You need something?"

Tori looked up at her friend and mentor. Drawing a deep breath, she allowed it to escape slowly before she began. *This's going to be harder than I thought.* "After the event is over, I'm leaving." She blurted the news out, hoping his reaction would be calm.

Stunned, he stood for a full minute considering her words in silence. He opened and closed his mouth a few times, as if the words were stuck, refusing to come out. Eventually he asked, "Is there a particular reason why?"

To this, Tori nodded, and tried to explain. "I'm emancipated. That means I don't need supervision, and I can go wherever I want."

He shifted his weight from one leg to the other, like he wanted to protest, but she cut him off with her hand, and continued, "Just hear me out, ok? What I mean is, I'm able to take care of myself, not that I want to go. But I *have* to go. I can't stay here. I've betrayed a very powerful organization. I got lucky with Enrique. His finding me could have turned out very ugly for me and for a lot of other people. I can't take that risk. You guys mean too much to me."

Tori paused for a moment, licking her lips anxiously. "You guys are like the family I never had. The last thing I want is to see any of you hurt because of me. The Organization would do that; they would hurt or kill people I care about just to get to me or to punish me."

She stopped there, seeing Terry's expression become grave. He knew what she was talking about. He had seen what bad men could and would do during his years as a Fed. He knew she was right; being there put everyone around her at risk.

"But there are always going to be people, Tori." He desperately wanted to change her mind. "No matter where you go, there are always people. We would look after you because we care about you. How do you know the people where ever you end up will do that for you?"

Tori shrugged, his logic somehow sounding flawed, as she had no intention of forming new relationships. She wanted to be alone, away from people. It would be the only way to make sure no one else paid the price for her actions. Besides, it was painful enough to leave. The last thing she wanted was to care about more people she would someday lose.

After a few more minutes of debate, Terry realized he wasn't going to change her mind. "Have you told anyone else?" he asked quietly.

She explained she did not think that would be a wise course of action. "It's imperative that no one know where I'm headed." She intended to slip away quietly. "I only thought it better to let you know since you will have to replace me."

Terry smiled at her thoughtfulness; *she realizes what her absence will mean.* He had come to care so much for her, it broke his heart that she intended to leave and never speak to him, or any of them, again.

Deep down, he knew this had been a difficult decision for his young charge, even though she chose what she believed to be right. He could not fault her for that, or for caring more for others than she did for herself. Nodding slowly, he asked, "What can I do?"

"Please tell everyone that I'll miss them. And tell them not to worry; I'm going to be ok." Stepping forward, she threw her arms around him, remembering the day they had met that she had refused to even shake his hand.

Rocking her back and forth, Terry stroked her long dark hair for several minutes. When he released her, he gave her a weak smile while fighting back the tears. He had never had any children, but for a brief time, she had been his little girl.

Nobody's Angel

Tori was a bundle of nerves the next day. The night before, while she drifted off to sleep, she had had a wickedly wonderful idea. She knew how to make sure Collin heard her song. The bad part though, everyone else would hear it, too.

When she arrived at work, she took the contestant list and added her own name at the bottom. She knew she couldn't win, but she wasn't going to let that stop her, as winning wasn't really the point. After she made the move, her nerves settled and she felt happy all day, knowing she'd get the chance to have her say.

The rules to the contest were very simple. A panel of judges from the record label would choose five finalists from the fifty who were going to play that day. Those five would return the following afternoon for the final round. The grand prize winner would play live on stage with *Indelible* at their opening concert for their tour that started in a few weeks. The winner would be announced at a private concert the band would be putting on at the store in three days.

The day started out fairly according to plan. Ten to twelve contestants played per hour, and things were right on schedule. They took an hour break at the halfway point for food and to give the judges a chance to rest and refresh. The young man who announced the contestants in turn had never been to the store during the set up and prep work that went into the event beforehand. Tori felt glad of this, as it increased the odds he would actually call her up, and she would make it onto the stage.

When the lunch break had ended, the band and judges returned from the back, where they had been resting in the stockroom. Tori had avoided going in there since she was currently on bad terms with two of the band members, and had focused on running the store.

While the next group of contestants performed, she began to pace behind the instrument counter, stealing peeks at her white beauty, the one that made her heart sing. When the list of names grew short, she unlocked the case and pulled it down, ready for her chance.

Terry observed her actions from the other counter, but did nothing, not really sure what to make of it. Tori took deep breaths, exhaling slowly and trying not to panic.

Finally, the last real contestant played on the tiny stage. Tori fluffed her hair and removed her jacket. She had worn a white tank top so she would not be overly warm, so her arms that were covered with scars were exposed and even her little Dragon mark showed. Today, she didn't care who saw them; they were her badges of survival, and she wore them with pride.

Grinning to herself, she knew she would sing her song, and it would explain it all. The contestant on stage finished, and her ebony locks bounced as she headed out of the booth and towards the front. An audible gasp went up from the crowd when the young man announced the final contestant.

Stepping onto the stage, Tori did not smile or wave, as many others had done. She simply snapped the lead into her guitar and adjusted the sound quickly. Ready to begin, she spoke into the mic, "Hey, Collin honey, this is for you," and she nodded in his direction.

Blasting her opening riff, she began her song that started out low, and no one moved to stop her from putting on her show. Her tone perfect, she belted out the lines she had written, first about her past and having grown up to do whatever men wanted, men who only used her because she was Nobody's Angel. During the chorus, Tori stole a glance around, and could tell most of the people were at least listening.

The second verse, she sang about not letting the booze touch her lips nor lying with men now that she could choose and say no, because she was still Nobody's Angel. This time for the chorus, she played a special riff that made her feel especially good as her fingers worked nimbly across the strings.

The final verse held the clincher, because she professed to be a murderer; a cold hearted bitch that would put you in the ground. And when she died, she knew she would do her time in hell, because, after all, she was Nobody's Angel. Again, she let loose with a lengthy burst of chords, then let the guitar drop as she ended the song and intended to get off the stage without another word.

However, some of the contestants had already been to the judge's table to protest her being allowed to compete; since she worked for the music store the conflict was clear. To head this off and try to appease everyone, the head judge himself had come to the stage to announce that Tori was not actually a contestant, and had no chance of winning.

Standing beside him as he made his little speech, Tori found she could not control herself and quipped into the mic, "Pfft, I already won." Looking him dead in the eye, she sneered, "I got the chance to play," and without waiting for anything else, she stepped off the platform, and made her way through the aisle, heading for the back and grabbing her jacket on the way by.

Some of the audience cheered for her while others were still upset, and a general chaos ensued. Tori pushed through the double doors, trying to catch her breath. Honestly, she could not believe she had made it through, and grinned profusely while she made her way to the office to have a moment of peace. Just before she reached it, a man stepped out in front of her.

For an instant, Tori stood frozen in place, staring at a dead ringer for Henry Morgan. Her mouth hung open momentarily before she snapped it closed, and she suddenly realized that she actually stood gaping at Michael Anderson, who simply said, "Hi."

Clenching her jaw, Tori had no intention of replying. Her heart had begun to race and panic paralyzed her lungs. *How the hell did he find me?* Her mind spun out of control. If Michael had found her, then God knows who else had. Instantly driven by fear, Tori simply handed him the guitar that she had been holding, shoving it at him more like, and made an about face, bolting back into the crowded sales floor.

She could hear him calling after her, but she did not look back. Terry fell in beside her as she pushed through the crowd, and as soon as they were outside, she told him she had to leave right that second. He followed her for long enough to hear her reasons for running and that she would not be back, as the man she was certain would follow her was trouble from her past. Turning around, he went back to catch the guy and detain him, hoping it would give her enough time to make her get away.

Looking back a few times, Tori did not see anyone behind her, and she ran all the way to the halfway house as fast as she could. She made it inside and did not bother to stop and catch her breath.

At her bursting through the kitchen, Sharon knew something had happened, and followed her upstairs to find out what. The girl had no time to explain, and simply grabbed her bag from under the bed and began throwing her things into it.

Sharon's face held utter shock when Tori pulled the pistol out from under the nightstand and shoved it into the bag. At that point, she grabbed the girls arms and insisted, "Tell me what the hell is going on!"

Deeply perturbed, Tori gave her the briefest explanation she could. "One of the men from years ago found me somehow. He was at the store tonight. He saw me, and he tried to corner me in the back. I have to leave. Now. If I don't, you could all be in terrible danger."

Sharon considered the girl's words as she stared at the black Nano sitting inside her bag, and demanded, "And how did you come by that?"

Tori released a loud, annoyed sigh. "I got it when Enrique first showed up, before I thought I could trust him. I don't really have time to explain how, I really have to go." She zipped the bag and threw it over her shoulder.

Sharon studied the younger woman's face for a moment, and then realized there would be no point in arguing. She was free to go if she wanted; the court had granted her that right. Quietly, she drew in a long breath, then asked in a motherly tone, "Well, since I can see there's no changing your mind, do you need anything before you leave?"

Tori thought for a moment, and then replied with a nod, "Yeah, I could use a ride."

Run Away

A few minutes later, Tori headed out to the grey Toyota that sat in the driveway. Tossing her bag into the back seat, she sat in the front, praying quietly to herself that they would get away and that her friends would be safe after she left. Sharon had stopped to tell her husband where they were going, and for a moment Tori thought they were going to fight over who would drive her.

Eventually, they decided that Brandon should stay with the house, in case the unwanted visitor turned up there, and Sharon would drive her to the bus station. He made his wife wait for a minute while Tori went on to the car, saying he needed to get something to send with her.

Anxiously, the girl waited. A nervous wreck, she thought she had everything she could possibly need; *let's GO*, she sighed. As if she had heard the command, Sharon came dashing out and jumped into the front seat beside her.

Driving straight to the bus station, Sharon parked the car and started to open the door as if she would go inside with her. But Tori stopped her, and insisted the older woman could not go; "It's time to say goodbye."

Tori fought to hold back the tears; the reason why she had wanted to sneak away, unseen, becoming clear. She did not want to face the fact she really wanted to stay in LA. An impossible notion, as tonight's events only proved she would be too easy to locate if she did.

"All right," Sharon agreed, "But hear me out before you

go. I have two things to tell you. First, we want you to come back whenever you can. Whenever it's safe or enough time has passed or whatever, we want you to come home. Second, we want to give you this." She held a small white envelope towards her.

Tori stared at it, speculating what she would find inside. Finally, she stammered, "I don't want your money."

"You don't have a choice. We insist. We know you don't have a lot saved up, and you're going to need something to get you started. So take it, please, and be on your way."

Sharon managed to smile, but Tori knew the woman cried inside. She knew it because she cried, too.

Reaching, she took the envelope with a trembling hand. It felt heavy in her grasp. Tucking it into the inside pocket of her jacket next to her lock pick set, she reached over and clung to her surrogate mother for a moment, and then stepped out into the evening sun, not looking back as she crossed the lot and headed into the terminal.

Once inside, Tori went straight over to the ticket counter to purchase her ticket. *I have to go to Denver.* She thought about jumping on the first bus to anywhere, just to get the hell out of town. *But surely they wouldn't find me here. Not this fast.*

Inquiring about the bus to Colorado, the ticket girl informed here there were many seats available, but it would be a two hour wait, as it would depart at 9:55 pm. Tori looked out the window at the setting sun and decided to wait for the right bus.

She purchased the ticket and headed out into the waiting area to find an out of the way spot to hunker down. She wanted to be able to see anyone coming before they got to her. Finally, she chose a bench that sat partially behind a tall building support, largely out of sight by anyone looking around. By laying over on it, Tori could see behind the pole as well as in front. She laid her bag on the bench and leaned on top of it, covering herself with newspapers from the neck down.

At a quarter to departure, Tori made her way to the bathroom. Doing her business, she began to grow tense, realizing that if anyone had found her, she would be confronted as she tried to board the bus. Trying to calm herself, she reached into her jacket and extracted the envelope. Inside, she discovered $5K in $100 bills; not the most she had ever seen, but the most that had ever been hers. Silently, she thanked her friends for their generosity and slipped the package back inside for safe keeping.

Not having any type of disguise, she would have to hope for the best. She pulled the pistol out of her bag and shoved it in her pocket, her pulse thumping loudly in her ears. Rubbing it gently, it brought her a small amount of comfort, recalling it had been the reason for choosing the bus over a plane; she would never have made it through security at the airport with it in her possession.

Heading outside, she got in line, and then climbed onto the transport. Swinging her gaze around the interior, she did not notice anything out of the ordinary. Making her way to her seat, she discovered she would be next to the window. Shoving her bag underneath, she placed her hand in her pocket with the pistol and stroked it lightly. Putting her elbow up against the glass, she covered her face so that no one would recognize her if they saw her from the outside.

Her breathing began to slow as she considered they were about to depart. She smiled to herself, joy at having made it away, while hoping her friends were safe and would not be harmed. Tori felt the brush of someone taking the empty seat beside her. Turning to see who her neighbor would be for the next eight hours, she felt her smile fall away as she looked squarely into the familiar face.

Sneak Peek at Entwined
Book 3 of A New Life Series

Glancing down at the number of the incoming call, Michael Anderson flipped open his phone, "Yeah."

"Hey, Mike, how you doin' little brother?" drawled a familiar male voice.

"Hey Henry, I'm good I guess. Long time no hear," his tone jovial, he sounded pleased to get word from his older sibling.

"Oh, ya know, life on the road. Listen, I gotta make this quick. Eddie's got a job that needs doin'. Was hopin' to put ya up for it."

"Eddie Farrell? Ah, you know I just got out a few months ago. Been thinking about finding a different way of life. Figure I got enough blood on my hands." Having worked with the group a couple of times in the past, Michael knew what his brother's crew, the Dragons, were into and had hoped to stay clear of it.

"Naw, man," Henry turned on the charm, "It's not a hit. Real easy job. Long term, too. He's got some guy he needs looked after. No blood and guts. Easy money."

Michael rocked his jaw side to side as he deliberated the offer. "Where you wanna meet?" he finally relented; *might as well, right?*

Henry released a quiet laugh. He knew his baby brother wouldn't say no. He gave him an address to a small bar in

Little Rock, "Two days from now, 'bout eightish, meet ya in the back."

Michael stared at the phone for a moment before returning it to his pocket, a dull ache in the pit of his stomach. *I always do what my big brother wants;* he sighed. *Someday, I'm gonna learn to make my own way. Just not today.*

Indelible

Peeking out through the swinging doors that led onto the sales floor, Michael could see his target standing inside the counter to his right, watching the contestants keenly. Allowing the door to close, he nervously walked away, knowing he would soon make his move.

He had noticed the girl a few days ago, when they had been in and out of the shop for the autograph session. Ever since then, he had been waiting, not so patiently, for the right time to make his presence known. *This is it,* he reassured himself. *Time for me to keep my word.* He knew he could ignore his promise, but then he would be letting his brother down. *Can't have that.*

Shuffling in a large circle, he continued to pace the floor. Stopping next to the work bench, he ran his fingers through his thick brown hair, his mind going over exactly what he would say for the umpteenth time.

It had been over four years since they last met, and he wasn't sure how she would take his suddenly showing up there, without any warning. His mouth dry, he licked at his lips anxiously. *God, I can't take this,* he thought to himself with a shake of his head. *I don't even like this girl. But Henry does...*

Once again at the double doors, he could see her making her way up to the stage, carrying a white guitar. Moving out into the crowd, he took a position next to the glass counter on the right. He panned the crowd; *this is a pretty tame group, considering*. Watching as she made it to the front, he leaned his rear end against the glass, tapping his boot anxiously.

Tori spoke into the mic, "Hey, Collin honey, this is for you," nodding in his direction.

Michael grinned at his employer's surprised expression, as he sat only a few feet from him at the moment. *Nice... this'll be good.* He had seen the girl in action back in the day. *Yeah, she's hot, if you like it nasty. I'm sure they had a real good time.*

Strumming the guitar, she began to sing. Her voice strong, she belted out the lines of her song, the first verse seeming to be about her past. Michael surveyed the crowd again, only half listening while watching for signs of trouble.

His mind shifted easily over the four days he spent with the Dragons; he recalled the group with a smirk. *I know exactly who and what she is... the kind of girl who enjoys spreading it around.* He folded his arms across his chest as he looked back towards the raised platform; *Nobody's Angel my ass.*

Hitting the second verse, she sang about not letting the booze touch her lips nor lying with men, because she was still Nobody's Angel. Michael chuckled. From what he had seen, he couldn't imagine a girl like that ever telling a man no. *Whatever you say, baby girl. Old habits die hard.*

Listening to the final verse, he felt his palms go sweaty, as she professed to being a murderer. *"I'm a cold hearted bitch... that'll put you in the ground... And when I die, I'll do my time in hell... because after all, I am... Nobody's Angel."* Her voice held deep emotion as her hands moved through the riffs.

Michael's blood ran cold. *Was that a threat?* Standing up straight, he could hear his pulse in his ears, pounding like a hammer, his eyes darting between Collin and the front of the crowd. *What the hell was that shit?* The Dragons were a horrific group of hired thugs, and she had been their whore; a typical needy woman from what he had seen. *Riding with them don't make you a badass, sweetheart.*

Entwined is Available Now!

About the Author

Anyone who knows me could tell you, I am a friendly kind of person, never met a stranger and take up conversations anywhere at any time. I work hard, and my mind never seems to shut down, as I wake up often in the middle of the night with ideas pouring out and demanding to be dealt with. Of course that means much of my books were written in the middle of the night.

I grew up and still live in the great state of Texas where everything is bigger, where we have warm weather and a central location. I love my state, my town, and my family, which includes my four sons, my significant other, and many friends as well.

I have thoroughly enjoyed writing this story and hope that you will love reading it just as much. And of course, there will be many more adventures to come.

You can follow Samantha Jacobey at:
Website: www.SamJacobey.com
Facebook: https://www.facebook.com/SamJacobey
Twitter: https://twitter.com/SamJacobey
Pinterest: http://www.pinterest.com/samanthajacobey/

Other works by Samantha Jacobey
http://www.amazon.com/-/e/B00GEB5LX0

Summer Spirit Novella Series - no one EVER had a summer romance like this... Charlie visits another plane, parallel to our own, where Summer Angels and Dark Angels battle over the fate of man. A unique twist on an old idea that will keep you guessing; will Charlie and Clarisse ever find their HEA? (New adult)

Irrevocable Series – from affluent beginnings, BAILEY DEWITT's life has become a broken mess... after her parents died unexpectedly, she didn't think it could get any worse. But when the arrogance of man catches up and puts the entire world into a dooms-day spiral, there will be only ONE PLACE she can run to... the ONE PLACE she wanted desperately to escape.... (New Adult)

Teach Me to Prey – in this standalone thriller, JASON TRUITT and his friends have gotten their way for years. Deceit, sex, and foul play aren't normally covered in the curriculum, but they're doing whatever it takes to get under BECKY STEWART's skin. When one of the boys turns up dead, it's a race against time to save the others; a STUNNING STORY that will get your heart racing and leave you breathless by the end... (New Adult)

The Wicked Awakened – a Halloween novel, a five hundred year old witch wants to turn SARAH MATTHEWS' body into her new home... A twisted tale involving a coven hell bent on seeing that she succeeds. Who will come out on top in this epic battle of wills? (Mature read, 18+ for sexual content and violence)